BARNSLEY LIBRARIES

CW00376284

THE

School

	Return Date	**Grimethorpe**
TH 4/00		12/15
22 SEP. 2000	07. AUG 04	09. FEB 16.
	13. DEC 04	
-5. MAR. 2001	02. SEP 06	
16. NOV. 2001		
26. JUL. 2002		
17. MAR. 2003	25. MAY 7.	
30. APR. 2003	20. AUG	
27. MAY 2003	06. OCT APR	
-4. JUL. 2003	8	

Grimethorpe

7/15

17. OCT. 2003

-2. JAN 2004

10. MAY 04   **10. DEC 15.**

LEASHED GUNS

In Bonanza they tried every way they knew to drive Luke Barron out of town. But Barron wasn't buying, not when there was range to bleed for, not when the wild bunch crowded him into a bushwhack canyon, not when he still had a round or two left in his .38.

Leashed Guns is a blazing story from the pen of one of the century's finest Western writers.

LEASHED GUNS

PETER DAWSON

A Black Horse Western

ROBERT HALE · LONDON

© 1992 by the Estate of Jonathan Hurff Glidden.
Published by arrangement with the
Golden West Literary Agency.

This edition 1992

ISBN 0 7090 4904 8

Robert Hale Limited
Clerkenwell House
Clerkenwell Green
London EC1R 0HT

Photoset in North Wales by
Derek Doyle & Associates, Mold, Clwyd.
Printed and bound in Great Britain by
WBC Print Ltd, and WBC Bookbinders Ltd,
Bridgend, Mid-Glamorgan.

ONE

The man on the grey reined off the trail a hundred yards below the big dead cottonwood. The sprawled litter of tarpaper and board shacks lining both sides of the canyon beyond the cottonwood took his momentary attention. The town would be Bonanza, he knew, for all along the trail below he had ridden the traffic of ore-wagons and lighter rigs, of men in the saddle and men afoot going in both directions, a few on the way out, more on the way in, the tell-tale signs of a boom-camp that still offered the promise of gold.

But after that first brief inspection, he ignored the town, his goal, in preference for the dead cottonwood, since there was something about it that held the eye. It had long ago shed its bark and the weather-whitened surface of trunk and gnarled branches showed plainly against the pale brown monotony of the sandy piñon-studded slope beyond. What was odd about this tree were the two rope-hung burdens dangling from its lowest

5

and thickest branch. It wasn't surprising that the cottonwood had served as a gallows, for it was the only sizeable tree the man on the grey had seen in the twelve long twisting miles that had brought him up this canyon that was watered by the mere trickle of a foot-wide stream. But it was odd that the bodies were placarded.

Flat on each dead man's chest, hung by a cord from each broken neck, the placards read identically LUKE BARRON BEWARE.

The lean face of the grey's rider turned grave a moment. Then a broad smile eased the severe planes of his features and he drawled under his breath, 'Now should I?'

Only then did he slowly look at the tent beneath the cottonwood and the man who stood in front of it and alongside a high board rectangle lined with rows of spikes. From this distance, the man on the grey could see that an odd assortment of weapons hung from those rows of spikes. There were six-guns, cartridge and cap and ball, long barreled and short, a few carbines, a pair of long rifles and two full rows of wicked-looking derringers and belly-guns. Along the front of the board was painted a sign: *Check your guns: Sheriff's Order*.

The cottonwood and the tent marked the place where traffic along the trail slowed and stopped. The man at the tent, a deputy evidently, inspected wagons and riders before waving them on. In the five minutes the man on the grey watched, he saw

6

several guns handed across to out-goers, several others taken from those on the way in.

He was faintly irritated by this show of authority. He had a week ago turned twenty-seven; but for ten of those years it had become his habit to keep a gun within reach both sleeping and waking. The prospect of now having to surrender the short-barreled .38 Colt that hung low in holster along his right thigh wasn't particularly welcome. Finally, when he moved on up the trail toward the cottonwood, he had decided he wouldn't surrender it.

He waited patiently while the deputy checked each passenger of an in-bound stage, collecting four six-guns and the driver's carbine. Then, it being his turn, he reined the grey in abreast the tent, looked across at the checking-board where the guns hung, and queried: 'Why all the trouble to de-horn the town?'

'Luke Barron,' the deputy said, as though the mention of that name should be answer enough.

'Who's he?'

'You ain't heard?' The deputy observed the stranger as though he was half-witted. 'You don't know Luke Barron? Hell, he's the biggest owl-hoot name this side of the Snake! Him and his wild bunch are operatin' around here.' ... He jerked his thumb over his shoulder to indicate the two bodies hanging from the limb behind him ... 'Them's two of his understrappers. Caught hijackin' claims night before last, hung at sun-up today. There's another ranny in jail now waitin' for the same medicine, Ed Tyler by name. Hand over your iron.'

The deputy suddenly made a stab to snatch the line of riders and wagons that had already formed behind this rider who seemed to be in no hurry. He was obviously not very fond of his job, which required that he stand out here in the full blaze of the sun; his face was glistening with perspiration and his shirt stuck wetly to his thick-muscled shoulders.

'Why should I?' the man on the grey queried.

The deputy's face took on a dark, ugly scowl. 'See here, stranger! I ain't in the habit of answerin' damn' fool questions! How do I know but what you're a Luke Barron man? How do I know but what you're Luke Barron hisself?'

'What if I am?'

The deputy moved his boots apart and stood with hands on hips. 'Salty, eh? You goin' to hand that iron across or do I take it off'n you?'

'I reckon I'll keep it,' the stranger drawled.

The deputy suddenly made a stab to snatch the stranger's weapon from holster. The stranger's right arm, idly bent across the horn of his saddle, straightened and seemed to move slowly. Yet the gun slid out from under the deputy's reaching hand with a half-second to spare. The stranger, tossing the weapon across to his left hand, rammed it through the waist-band of his denims out of the deputy's reach, stating, 'You can get along without mine.'

'Like hell! Hand it over!' All his patience gone, the deputy made a grab for the grey's reins. The animal jerked his head away, roared, and settled placidly onto all four hooves again as the deputy scrambled wildly out of the way, tripping on a tent-rope and sprawling on his back.

He rolled over quickly, hat falling into the dust. When he sat up his right hand was swinging a gun up from holster. But his arm froze in the act of lining his weapon. For he was staring into the round bore of the stranger's .38. He dropped his gun as though it was scorched too hot to hold by the pitiless glare of the sun.

'No offense taken,' the stranger drawled. 'Now if you'll kindly step wide of that hog-leg and walk off there a few steps, I'll be on my way.'

The deputy, his face gone purple with rage, picked himself up, then his Stetson and beat the dust from it; he was careful to stay away from his gun lying nearby. He had enough sanity left him to recognize a quality of warning in the stranger's smooth tone and walked ten feet out from the tent, his look ugly as he caught the raucous laughter of an ore-wagon driver who was waiting his turn far down the line. Others immediately joined in a derisive demonstration against him, and when the stranger said, 'A bit further,' he swore obscenely as he doubled the distance between him and the tent.

'Just wait there till I'm clear,' the stranger said, sheathing his weapon in a swift effortless motion of practiced ease. He lifted his reins and put the grey on up the trail.

Entering the lower end of the street ten rods beyond, the stranger looked back to see the deputy run to his gunrack and lift down a carbine. He reined the grey in behind the protection of a passing buckboard and went on, ignoring the threat of the rifle back there.

TWO

Bonanza was an ugly town under the sun's pitilessly hot midday glare. There was nothing permanent about the shacks that lined its narrow muddy street which was the bed of the canyon. A third of the dwellings at the upper end were tents. At first the presence of the filth and mud and stagnant pools of water along the street puzzled the stranger; then he saw the sluices of the diggin's up beyond the town limits and knew that they must be leaking badly or that their owners were careless of the water. Up the gradual slope of the east wall was a dug ditch that he rightly concluded must carry the scant waters of the stream around the town. High on the rim of the west wall stood a huge redpainted water tank and alongside it a windmill.

The walks at the town's center were crowded, jammed with a restless-moving assortment of rich and poor, a mass of seedy-looking and rough-shod men and occasionally one that was immaculately outfitted. There were few women and most all of these were profuse of powder and rouge, the plainest sign of the lusty bawdiness of this new boom-camp. There were more saloons and gambling houses than stores. They were all doing a full-out business. The street was jammed with a varied collection of light and heavy rigs and saddlehorses wading fetlock deep in the mud. Bonanza had the wide-open look of all boom-camps, the only contradiction being the stand beneath the cottonwood at the foot of the street. Not a gun was in sight.

The man on the grey reined into a narrow vacant space at a tie-rail before a saloon, the *Nugget*, witnessing the strangest of all the sights Bonanza boasted. Forming a long line out onto the street waited half a hundred men, women and children, all carrying pails or buckets or any receptacle that would hold water. At one corner of the *Nugget*'s flimsy frame wall stood a gun-belted man wearing a badge like the one the stranger had seen on the deputy back at the cottonwood. At knee height on the wall beside this second deputy protruded the stem of a pipe, and at the pipe's end was a thick valve. The ground close by was sticky with mud. Against the wall sat a nail keg with a slit in its top.

The stranger saw the deputy fill a woman's pail, collect a coin from her and drop it through the slit in the keg, then hurriedly push her out of the way so he could serve the next customer. He was selling water.

Curious, the stranger looked beyond the saloon and up toward the rim where he'd seen the water-tank. Down from the tank, following the natural line of a gully, he could see the pipe line that ended here at the walk. More than curious now, he reached down and tapped the shoulder of a wide-hatted figure passing his stirrup toward the walk, asking, 'What's goin' on here?'

The head lifted and the stranger was looking into a girl's pretty oval face. He was surprised, for the Stetson and the man's waist overalls and the plain cotton shirt had given him no warning that he was addressing a woman.

She told him, her face touched by a wry smile: 'You must be new here. This is Matt Geis's well. He's selling water. Twenty-five cents a pail, two dollars and a half a barrel. Cheap, isn't it? Matt Geis is a public benefactor. Without his well, we'd all have died of typhoid long ago!'

Her biting sarcasm wasn't lost upon the stranger. Yet he was more alert to the contra-diction of that sarcasm, her finely turned features, the pale blonde hair that framed the face and the direct eyes that were the blue of a deep mountain lake.

He reached up to touch the brim of his Stetson, smiling now, drawling, 'I reckon that answers the question. This Matt Geis must be a powerful good friend of yours.'

'He is not!' the girl flared, unamused by his effort to match her sarcasm. Suddenly her glance took in the gun low along his thigh. He saw her face lose color. Then she was saying in a biting voice: 'You knew all along! You're one of Sam Ingels' deputies.'

'Beggin' your pardon, I ain't, ma'am.'

Now her glance showed alarm. 'Then how … then why are you wearing a gun?'

'Because I always tote one.'

She glanced quickly to the walk, as if wanting to make sure she couldn't be overheard. Then, low-voiced, she told him: 'You'll be arrested unless you hide it! It's against the law to carry one within the town limits.'

With that, she turned and left him, going hurriedly to the walk and along it until she was lost in the crowd.

The stranger sat watching her until she was out of sight. His glance came back to the deputy who waited on his customers. With a shrug, he swung lithely down out of the saddle and looped the grey's reins over the hitch-pole and sauntered in through the crowd to the *Nugget*'s swing doors. He was thinking mainly of the girl, wondering who she was and if he'd ever see her again.

Ten minutes later, elbowing the crowded varnished bar in the saloon, he was lifting a shot-glass of bourbon to his mouth when he felt the jab of a gun's hard snout along his backbone.

14

Behind him, someone drawled, 'Hold it, stranger! You're under arrest!'

The weight of the .38 eased off his thigh. He calmly set his glass back on the bar as the voice said again, more crisply, 'Reach! Turn around, slow!'

The stranger's hands lifted to shoulder level. With the gun still ramming his spine, he started turning to the right until he could feel it no longer. In a brief instant he had a glimpse of the cottonwood deputy, gun holstered, and a massively-built man outfitted in black broadcloth and a white shirt. The man with the gun at his back wasn't within his range of vision.

Lazily, but with the same swift sureness the deputy had seen earlier in his draw, the stranger brought his right elbow back and down in a hard stab. The point of his elbow caught the man behind full in the face. The blow, vicious, knocked the man's head sideways. Before he could recover, the stranger's hand had swept on down and caught his wrist a slashing stroke that spun the gun from his hand. The stranger caught the gun in mid-air, threw it quickly into line with the deputy and his companion, raised a boot and put all his weight into its thrusting drive.

Just as his boot took his victim in the pit of the stomach, the stranger saw the sheriff's badge pinned on the man's vest-pocket. Then the boot struck. The sheriff staggered backward and fell and slid across the sawdusted floor. Pushing himself up on one elbow, rage plain on his moustached face, he ignored the gun in the stranger's hand and snatched out the stranger's .38 he had a moment ago thrust into his belt.

The stranger arced the .45 around and thumbed one shot. The sheriff gave a grunt of pain, his hand opened and he dropped the .38 to the floor. Across the outside of his wrist was a red line where the bullet had scorched him.

He snarled, 'Get him, Jack!'

But the deputy to whom he'd spoken kept his hand carefully clear of his gun.

The third man, the one in the broadcloth suit, gave the stranger a searching glance. He obviously didn't share the deputy's and the sheriff's anger. All at once a smile broke across his loose-jowled face and he said, 'Sam, we need this man!'

Sheriff Sam Ingels came awkwardly to his feet, pointedly ignoring the gun lying near him on the floor and standing hunched over from the pain in his stomach where the stranger's boot had taken him. He gave the man in broadcloth an uncomprehending look, saying flatly, 'You gone loco, Matt?'

Matt Geis, owner of the *Nugget*, owner of Bonanza's sole water supply, nodded toward the back of the room. 'Let's talk this thing over,' he said, and nodded to the stranger. 'You, too.' He turned and started back along the bar, ignoring the bystanders who had watched the swift happenings of the past moments with unadulterated satisfaction.

Sam Ingels eyed the stranger levelly for a moment, rubbing his miraculously uninjured wrist. The stranger was leaning on the bar again, the sheriff's .45 hanging in his hand at his side, waiting. The sheriff said curtly to his deputy, 'Get back out there, Jack!' Then, as the deputy left, he spoke to the stranger, nodding toward the saloon-owner's departing back: 'Go ahead.'

'You go ahead.'

The sheriff's face colored deeply as his anger returned. But he thought better of saying whatever was on his mind and turned without a word to follow Geis. The stranger walked over, picked up his .38, wiped the sawdust from it, and sauntered back along the room after the other two.

Stepping into the office last, he closed the door behind him and tossed the sheriff's .45 across the room into a deep leather chair.

Matt Geis's broad smile showed again. 'Sam, you've hired a new deputy.'

'Who?' the stranger asked.

'You.'

Sam Ingels growled sullenly, 'I'll choose my own men, Matt!'

Geis replied flatly, 'Take him across and give him a badge.'

The lawman shrugged his shoulders and made no answer, making it obvious that Geis was in the habit of giving him orders and he of obeying them.

Geis said, 'The pay's good, stranger. There's a bonus besides. What's your handle?'

'Luke Barron.'

The saloon-owner's booming laugh rang against the walls of the small room. 'Sure. Mine's Wyatt Earp.' Then, seeming not to care what the stranger's real name was, he went on, 'All right, Luke it is. Here's the setup, Luke. You get a hundred a month from the county. What you get from me depends on how much you bring in.'

'How much what?'

Geis made an impatient gesture with one hand. 'Sam'll put you wise to how we run things. The point is, will you take the job?'

'No.'

'You'll have to. Me and Sam and his deputies are the only ones allowed to pack guns inside the town limits.'

'I've still got mine.'

Geis chuckled, his voice low-toned, coarse. He was a big man, gone slack with middle age and easy living. But there was about him a hint of brute strength even for his ample paunch and the looseness of his face. His eyes, coal-black, were alive and alert. Once more those eyes seemed to size up this stranger. 'So you have, Luke. We'll let you keep it on condition you work for us.'

The stranger took a sack of tobacco from his vest pocket and built a smoke. After lighting it, he drawled, 'You rannies haven't yet backed a threat with anything I should worry about. But name your proposition. I'll listen.'

'I've already named it,' Geis told him. 'A hundred in salary, a bonus besides.'

'What's the bonus?'

'Two hundred, four hundred a month. Maybe more, accordin' to how you handle it.'

The stranger whistled softly. 'Real money, eh?'

Geis nodded.

'Any strings attached?'

'None. Only you play the cards the way we deal 'em, Luke.'

The stranger was silent for a long moment. All at once he asked, 'This Luke Barron scare is a fake, then?'

His question took Matt Geis unawares. For a moment the saloon-owner's eyes showed faint alarm. Then they veiled over into inscrutability and he said, 'You're goin' at this too fast, Luke. Either you're in or you're out. Which'll it be?'

'I reckon I'm in.'

THREE

At midnight, Bonanza's street was as alive as it had been at three this afternoon or at nightfall. The saloons were open, the walks were crowded, there was noise and confusion. The stranger decided to wait no longer to set out on an errand he had hoped to carry out while the town slept. It was plain now that Bonanza never slept, wakefulness being a virtue it boasted as do all boom-camps.

The *Nugget* and its foul reek of tobacco smoke and stale beer behind him, he drew deep lungfuls of chill night air and found it a bracer to keep him awake. Today had been his fourth in the saddle and he yearned to ride on up into the hills, unlace the blankets from his saddle and allow himself the luxury of a night's uninterrupted sleep. But he had something more important than sleep on his mind and, characteristically, he set about doing it.

Opposite and down-street from the *Nugget* was the stage-station and its feed-barn where he'd earlier left the grey. He went across there and asked a stable hand: 'Got a room with bath up in the loft?'

'Two-bits'll buy the whole thing for the night,' was the man's answer.

The stranger handed over a quarter, went back to unlace his blanket from his saddle and, carrying the blanket, climbed the ladder into the loft. Up there he noisily set about raking up loose hay for a bed; he moved a bale out of the way, ungently, letting it fall heavily so that it made the loft floor-planking creak. Catching the sounds from below, the stable-hand presently was sure that his lone night lodger had finally made himself a bed and turned in for the night.

The stranger waited ten more minutes before he soundlessly came down the loft ladder and moved through the shadows along the wagon-lot and into the alley at its rear. He took the alley up-street, circling out of it once to avoid light coming from the broad rear windows of a saloon almost opposite the *Nugget*. Past three more buildings, he came abruptly upon the rear of Bonanza's jail.

Earlier, this afternoon, he had become well acquainted with the front of the jail, where Sheriff Sam Ingels had his office. And from the street he'd looked along a passageway back toward the alley, his brief glance more searching than would have been apparent to the casual observer. Now, in the darkness, he picked out details he'd firmly sealed in his mind in that one fleeting glimpse.

Here, to the south of the jail, Bonanza's first brick building, the bank, was taking shape. Its walls were already above the height of its single-story stone neighbor. Close by along the alley was a water barrel, an overturned mortar box, sacks of cement and a huge stack of neatly-piled brick that must have cost the bank directors a young fortune to haul in from the rail-head, thirty miles away. Above, at the corner nearest the jail, the long shadowy line of a strong derrick-boom angled up over the wall's edge. This boom was used to lift mortar and brick to the scaffolding inside the rising new walls. Down from the boom hung a stout inch-and-a-half rope with a hook at its end. Directly under the hook was a small stack of thirty or more bricks already in its cradle of steel-cables that was used for hoisting it above. The workmen had quit tonight ready to hoist that load of brick to the workings on the scaffolding.

The stranger's glance took this in casually, among other things, chief of which was a waist-high saw horse that he sauntered over to pick up and carry to the rear wall of the jail, placing it directly under the one small barred window of the stone wall.

Regardless of Bonanza's other temporary features, its jail had been built to last. It was as close to being break-proof as man could make it. The stone walls were two feet thick, of rimrock cut to fit closely to make the walls impregnable. The roof was likewise strong, if the office roof as the stranger remembered it was anything to judge by. Foot-thick logs were covered with boards, then several inches of dirt and finally, he judged, a tarpaper roof. The chimneys, he guessed again, would be the only openings to the roof.

He stood on the saw-borse and found that his head came even with the inch-thick rock imbedded bars of the window that was too small to permit the passage of a man's shoulders. He picked up a shard of stone from the window-ledge, tossed it inside, and called softly, 'Ed!'

He heard the creak of a cot in a cell toward the front. Then a voice answered in a hushed explosive exclamation: 'Luke!'

Luke Barron said, 'Big as life, Ed.'

'Damned if I thought you'd even get here!' came Ed Tyler's low words from inside. Then, ruefully, Luke Barron's lieutenant added, 'Looks now like you couldn't do me any good anyway. They string me up to that cottonwood below town at sun-up tomorrow.'

'I know all about it. Maybe you won't be here at sun-up.'

'This ain't the time for jokin', Luke.'

'I mean it! I'm goin' to bust you out.'

'Yeah? How?'

Luke Barron ignored the disbelief in his friend's voice: 'Light a match and show me the layout inside.'

A match had flared in there. It outlined Ed Tyler's short compact form standing near the door of the far cell toward the front. A corridor, with this window at its rear, ran along the left side of the jail to the steel-faced door leading to the sheriff's office. To the right were three cells, Ed Tyler in the one at the corridor's office end.

Luke let out a long worried sigh. This was going to be tougher than he'd thought at first. The cells were enclosed by bars as thick as the ones at this window. The walls couldn't be broken down. The roof was sturdy. He wished now that he had clubbed the sheriff, taken his keys and let Ed Tyler walk out the unlocked door of his cell.

Or did he? No, he told himself, *Ed had to get out of there without anyone knowin' who got him out … if we're going to get to the bottom of this other thing, this Luke Barron sandy someone is takin' the trouble to frame on me.*

The match inside guttered out and Ed called, 'Fat chance you got of gettin' me out. This layout was built for keeps!'

'The roof's droppin' in on you in about a minute,' Luke said on quick impulse. He had just seen the line of the timbers running crosswise to the long room, also the stone wall separating the jail from the office in front. 'You'd better stand close to that

24

wall. Wrap a blanket around your head. When the roof's open, climb up the rope.'

'What rope?'

'There'll be one,' Luke answered. He jumped down off the saw-horse and carried it back to its place at the rear of the new bank.

Now that he'd found a barely possible way of getting Ed Tyler out of jail, he was eager to be at it. He stepped up to the cable-slung pile of brick, trying to lift it. It was a dead weight that he couldn't budge and that satisfied him.

He reached up for the hook dangling from the rope of the derrick-boom. Pulling it down to him, he breathed more freely when the absence of any creaking from above told him that the hoisting mechanism of the derrick was well-oiled. He fastened the hook to the cable-sling of the pile of bricks, took a last look along the alley to make sure no one was about, then mounted the ladder to the top of the wall.

The mortar-littered scaffolding ran ten feet high inside the four walls. In from the wall flanking the jail stood the sturdy vertical stem of the derrick, a cable from its top holding the swinging boom in place. On the platform of the derrick that was scaffold-high was the cable drum and two sets of cogged wheels, both turned by long-handled cranks. One, the smallest, was for regulating the height of the boom. The other, geared to the drum, was for hoisting the load.

Luke gingerly turned the hoist-handle. The oiled mechanism worked smoothly, almost soundlessly. It was quiet enough not to be detected for the street out front was giving off its restless undertone of perpetual noise, the sound of raucously raised voices, the jingle of wagon harness and the shouts of the barkers at the saloon-entrances.

He cranked the hoist until the heavy load of brick swung into sight beyond the shadow of the rear wall. He brought the load higher, then reached up and swung the boom around until the load of brick hung over the jail roof. He was thankful that the rock wall separating office and jail made a slight bulge along the flat roof. Otherwise, he couldn't have been sure where the enormous weight of the brick was to fall.

By turning one crank, then the other, he finally had the suspended load of brick where he wanted it. The long derrick boom held it twenty feet above the roof. He leaped the passageway and went onto the jail roof and looked directly upward, making a small adjustment in the boom's angle when he returned so as to be sure the brick hung over a spot he judged to be between two of the roof-joists as he remembered them from his glimpse as Ed held the match.

Satisfied, he eased the drum-handle over a bare inch, tipped the ratchet that locked the gears, and let go the handle. Holding his breath, he caught the whirr of the drum as it suddenly unwound. The brick-load started falling slowly. Then it gathered speed and plummeted down toward the roof.

FOUR

The stacked bricks hit with the exploding sound of both barrels of an eight-gauge being fired at once. The flat surface of the roof gave way, the brick going on through as though falling through cardboard. The sound of splintering timbers echoed up out of the opening and the scaffolding on which Luke stood trembled as though the ground was threatening to shake these new walls down. Out of the hole rose a cloud of dust. He saw the rope sway and suddenly tighten. Then Ed Tyler was climbing hand over hand up out of the hole. Luke pulled the boom on around and once more released the drum catch to lower Ed into the alley.

The whole thing, from the moment of his releasing the ratchet to dropping Ed into the alley, had been accomplished in the space of half a dozen breaths.

He jumped down off the wall instead of using the ladder. Shouts were echoing in off the street

28

and all at once he heard the slam of the sheriff's office door. He said urgently, 'This way!' and turned up the alley at a run, Ed's quick boot-tread pounding behind.

A few doors above the jail, he cut out at right angles from the alley, climbing the uneven slope of the canyon wall toward the rim. Halfway to the rim, he halted, breathing hard, and let Ed come up with him.

Ed's square homely face shaped a broad smile. He lifted a hand and ran it around his short-coupled neck. He drawled, 'Thanks for keepin' this all in one piece!'

'Forget it!' Luke sat on a nearby low outcropping. He waited until his lungs weren't quite so crowded, thankful for his luck and the presence of this man who had been like a brother to him for almost ten years now. Then, seeing shadowy figures moving along the alley by the jail and the dim glow of a lantern on its roof, he said urgently: 'There isn't much time. I've got to get back down there in case they start lookin' for me. So let's have it in a hurry. How come you wound up in that *jusgado*?'

'Like I said in the letter. After you headed back for the Brazos with your pardon, I ...'

'You told me that,' Luke interrupted. 'You thought you saw a chance to take in some suckers at cards and came up here. What went wrong?'

'I picked the *Nugget*, a joint down the street,

and opened up a friendly stud game one night. Matt Geis, who owns the place, saw through my game and called the sheriff. They locked me up. Couple of days later the sheriff ran onto that old reward-dodger with my picture on it. Before that he was goin' to let me go. When he found out I was one of your bunch, he …'

'But you wrote the letter before you went to jail, didn't you? You told me how a wild bunch up here was framin' all their night ridin' on me.'

'That's right. I got the story on the way in, before I ever laid eyes on the town. How Luke Barron's gang had this town and the diggin's by the tail. So I wrote you and sent the letter back with the driver of the stage I came in on. Then, when Ingels found out I was one of your men, it gave him ideas. Did you happen to notice two jaspers hangin' from a cottonwood just below town?'

'You can't very well miss 'em.'

'Well, that's the idea I gave Ingels … him and whoever else is behind this frame-up. They had me, a genuine Luke Barron man. It was a cinch they couldn't turn me loose. The sheriff had a couple deputies who were gettin' a little too salty to suit him … emptyin' the claim-owner's pokes on their own, I reckon. When he saw he'd have to get rid of me, it gave him the idea of how to handle his deputies. He arrested 'em, had 'em tried. They were identified as two of a gang that had raided the diggin's a few nights previous. So the sheriff let it get around they were your men. When a mob stormed the jail, he surrendered his keys. Those two jaspers lived about ten minutes after I saw the mob lead 'em away.'

Luke fitted Ed's story to the picture he already had of the way Sam Ingels and Matt Geis were operating under the use of his name. Until now, he had had little to go on but what Geis had said in the *Nugget* today ... Ingels had later been close-mouthed about his duties as a deputy. Ed's story added conviction to what he already suspected. Those two, Matt Geis and Sam Ingels, were obviously the leaders of a gang that was terrorizing Bonanza and the diggin's under the name of Luke Barron.

He asked, 'How come they didn't invite you to join their necktie party?'

'The sheriff kept his mouth shut about me. I figured he was savin' me until later. The hunch was correct. Night before last a bunch of jaspers hit the diggin's and helped themselves to every ounce of gold they could lay hands on. Two claim-owners were shot down when they tried to argue. There was hell to pay. The town went loco. Then, this mornin', the sheriff announced he'd arrested me after turnin' me loose two days ago. He had my reward-dodger and told who I was, Luke Barron's right bower. They took me to court and the trial took about five minutes. You should

have been here to see Ingels and his men gettin'
me back to jail. The mob was yellin' for blood. So
the sheriff parleyed with 'em and promised a
hangin' for sun-up in the mornin'. There you have
it.'

Luke took a deep drag on his smoke and
exhaled slowly. He reached into a vest-pocket and
took out his deputy's badge, handing it across to
Ed. 'See what I picked up today.'

Ed whistled softly. 'Where'd you find it?'

'Didn't find it. Ingels pinned it on me.'

'You! A deputy!' Suddenly Ed was laughing,
long, loudly.

'Quiet, or you'll have 'em up here after us,' Luke
cautioned, and briefly explained how he came to
have the badge. He ended by saying, 'So we're one
jump ahead of Geis. Unless I'm 'way wrong, he's
the Big Augur in this. But we'll have to move fast.
I'll work along with him and be in touch with you
at the same time. You've got to round up a handful
of honest men, tell them what we're doin', and sell
them on the idea of fightin' Geis. They're not to
know who I am.'

'Fight! With what?' Ed asked ruefully. 'Every
gun inside the town limits is out there at the tent
under the cottonwood. We can't go against Matt
Geis with sling-shots!'

'We'll get guns, don't worry.'

Ed Tyler's homely face took on a wide grin as he
heard this calm statement. He was as unlike Luke

Barron in physical appearance as any man could
be, a head and a half shorter, thick-bodied and as
dark as Luke was blond. But they had one thing in
common; an ingrained recklessness bred of years
on the dark trails, a quick-wittedness long trained
in fighting trouble. Luke seemed to have no
nerves and when he moved it was with a studied
almost indolent ease that was deceptive and sure.
Ed was different, quick-muscled, nervous, proud
of a hair-trigger temper.

Just now Ed was relishing Luke's last statement, which was symbolic of the outlaw's
readiness to do the impossible. If they needed
guns, Luke would get guns. It was as simple as
that, as simple as most of the precarious living of
their past ten years. The companionship that had
sprung up between them was of two unlike minds,
each somehow grooved to work smoothly with the
other. Luke, outlawed from Texas for a killing in
self-defence, had recently received a deserved
pardon and headed back for the Brazos. Ed, an
inveterate gambler, who had time and again been
in hot water over his liking for marked cards, was
born to the owl-hoot trail, as Luke wasn't. For ten
years they'd sided each other, not as outlaws but
as men trying to earn an honest living at running
cattle back in the Colorado hills where the law
was lax and a man's life depended on his guts and
his quickness of hand to gun. It was no fault of
Luke's that they had become involved in a range

war and that his name had been spread in blazing headlines when the small ranchers, under his leadership, had made the range-hogs eat crow. It was no fault of his now that Matt Geis and Sam Ingels chose to use his well-known name to hide behind.

'Somethin' I can't get straight,' Ed drawled, 'is why they'd pick your name to travel under when you've got your pardon, when they might know you've headed for home.'

'Maybe they don't know about the pardon.'

Ed shrugged and stood up from the outcropping, frowning, looked down onto the alley where a crowd had formed at the rear of the jail. He said finally, 'Layin' hands on these honest men, as you call 'em, is goin' to be a tough job. The only friend I've got is an old jasper name of George Randall that I kept from gettin' cleaned that first night in the game in the *Nugget*. He staked out the original claims up here, discovered the placers. Geis won his claims in a crooked game one night about four months ago. Since then, until his daughter turned up about a week ago, he'd been eatin' and sleepin' with a bottle, tryin' to forget. He's about as useful as a crutch would be to a bronc-rider.'

'If he nurses a grudge against Matt Geis, we can use him.'

Ed's frown tightened. 'So them's the kind of jaspers you want, eh? Then Doc Savage would be another. He's tried for weeks to tell the council there'll be a typhoid epidemic here unless the town gets good water to drink. Anyone tell you about Matt Geis's well?' He caught Luke's answering nod and continued: 'So far they haven't listened to Savage. He even went to Geis and asked for free water for those who couldn't buy it. Geis had him thrown out of the saloon.'

'Then there's your second man. Get me half a dozen like Randall and Savage and we can stake Geis's hide out to dry.' Luke flicked his cigarette away, watching its shower of sparks as it struck the ground below them. 'Where'll I find you tomorrow night?'

'At Randall's shack at the diggin's, I reckon,' Ed said. 'You can't miss it. It's up the west slope, away from the others. If I'm not there, Randall or his daughter will tell you where I am.'

'Then let's be movin',' Luke drawled, noticing that the crowd at the jail had moved from the alley out onto the street now.

Ten minutes later three men tramped up the ladder to the stage-station loft. Luke stood up suddenly from behind a bale of hay that was between his blanket and the loft-opening. Although he hadn't been lying there more than a quarter minute, his hair was mussed and his eyes squinted into the glare of a lantern. The lantern was carried by the deputy who had been at the tent under the cottonwood this morning.

Luke said sharply, 'Do you have to make all that noise?'

'Just checkin' up to see if you were here,' the deputy replied. 'You been asleep?'

'No. Been countin' my toes here in the dark.' Luke's right hand lifted into sight and he laid his .38 on the bale of hay ahead of him.

The deputy's glance took in the gun. 'Someone busted a prisoner out of jail. We're huntin' him.'

'Meanin' you thought I busted him out?' Luke drawled. 'Maybe I did. Maybe I came up the ladder right ahead of you.'

The deputy smiled meagrely, well aware that he couldn't afford to lose his temper under Luke's taunting words. 'Hit the hay again, stranger,' he said. 'If you've been on your feet since you came in here an hour ago, it's been sleep-walkin'.' He nodded to his two companions and the three of them filed back down the ladder.

Luke, lying back on his blanket, relishing the pleasing flow of weariness that settled along his flat muscles, smiled faintly into the darkness. He was asleep before that smile had gone from his face.

FIVE

Matt Geis's first words to Sam Ingels the next morning in the *Nugget* office, were, 'Where's the new man?'

'Loafin' out front by the water line.' The lawman's narrow face wore a worried look. 'I'd sure as hell like to know who broke that roof in last night.'

'Did Tyler have a partner when he hit town?'

Ingels shook his head.

'Who did he know here?'

'No one I know of. He came in on the stage the day you had him arrested. Afterwards, I heard he saved George Randall from losin' his shirt in that stud game that night. You reckon they're acquainted?'

'Even if they are, Randall wouldn't have the guts to pull a job like that jailbreak.'

'He might, now that that girl of his has sobered him up. They say he's a new man.'

Matt Geis waved the idea aside. 'A man don't

get his guts back that quick. What about Luke?'

'Luke? Oh, the new deputy. Ray found him asleep in the loft over at the stage-station right after it happened. It wasn't him.'

Geis tilted back in his swivel-chair behind the mahogany desk. He was remembering the new deputy and how quickly he had turned the tables on Sam Ingels out at the bar yesterday. Now he laughed softly to himself, for a man with the stranger's blunt arrogance talked Geis's language.

On abrupt impulse, he said, 'Get Luke in here. I'm going to tell him the set-up.'

'The whole thing? About the hideout up the canyon?' ... Ingels shook his head ... 'Better go easy before you tip your hand, Matt.'

'Why?'

The lawman shrugged. 'We're trustin' enough men as it is. Figure out another way of usin' this stranger. After all, what do we know about him?'

'What do we know about any of these hard-cases you've hired? Hell, you've spooked over nothin', Sam!'

'Who said I was spooked?' Ingels grumbled belligerently.

'He's the pick of the bunch, Luke is. He's got a brain. The others haven't. Get him in here and I'll show you.'

The sheriff made an outflung helpless gesture with his hands and reluctantly left the office to follow the saloon-owner's order. In the interval he was gone, Matt Geis took a cigar from a box on the desk, lit it and rocked back in his chair enjoying the rich aroma of the weed. He decided finally that there might be more than a grain of common sense in his sheriff's advice. They were trusting a lot of men with the knowledge of what was going on here. Those two men hanging from the cottonwood below town had known what was going on and tried to over-step the bounds of Matt Geis's authority. 'Guess I'd better go slow on this,' he thought.

When the door opened to admit first the sheriff, then the new deputy, Geis said affably, 'Howdy, Luke. Have a chair.' He indicated a high-backed ornate chair that stood along the wall. Then he caught the expression of pale anger on Sam Ingels' face. 'What's the matter? You two have another run-in?'

'He was givin' away water!' Ingels flared.

Geis's glance swung sharply on Luke. His new well was his pride; anything out of the way about its operation touched him on a sore spot. 'How about it?' he asked sharply.

'An old woman out there found she'd lost her pocket-book when it came time to pay. Your man had filled her pails. When he saw he wasn't goin' to get paid, he started dumpin' the water into the street. I made him step aside while I filled her pails again and let her go after she'd promised to bring the money this afternoon.'

Geis's belligerent frown eased a trifle. He looked at Ingels. 'See, Sam, it ain't as bad as you think.'

'She'll never turn up with that money,' the lawman flared.

'What if she doesn't?' Geis shrugged. 'Losin' two pails of water won't break me.' ... He looked sharply at Luke ... 'But don't try anything like that again! Men who work for me go along the way I say or ...'

He let his unworded threat carry into the room's stillness for a brief moment before he reached for the box of cigars, opened it, and offered it first to the sheriff, then Luke. 'Here, you two. Light up. Bury the hatchet. We've got something to talk over.'

Ingels took a handful of cigars and went to a chair in the corner of the room. Luke refused one with a brief negative shake of his head and leaned back against the wall, arms folded across his wide chest.

Looking at this tall blond man whose gun-belt sagged awkwardly low at his flat thigh, Matt Geis made a mental reservation, which was to keep the truth of his doings to himself. He pegged Luke now as a man who might rebel at an outright admission of dishonesty but one who would play the game to its end so long as the obvious was kept under cover. He searched a moment for a way to explain things to his new man, but couldn't find one. However, he was a past master at playing for time and now he began doing that, hoping an idea would come to him:

'Luke, you've got some mistaken ideas on what we're doin' here. You asked yesterday if this Luke Barron scare's a fake. To tell the truth, we don't know. Last night Ed Tyler, one of Barron's men, was busted out of jail. That makes it look like the thing might be genuine after all. But let's forget Luke Barron.

'What's more important is that we've got a town here where easy money's ripe for the pickin'. Luke Barron may be getting his. I see to it I get mine. One way is charging for water from my well. It cost me better than a thousand to sink that well. I've got my money back ten times over. At the same time, I'm runnin' a legitimate business.'

Geis hesitated at something he saw about Ingels' new deputy. Suddenly he asked: 'Where's your badge?'

Luke fished into a vest pocket and produced his deputy's shield. 'Here.'

'Why aren't you wearin' it?'

'Figured I might live longer if I didn't. These people here don't seem to waste much love on the law.'

Geis smiled broadly, shooting a glance at the sheriff to see his moustached face coloring once more in anger. 'You ain't worn it since you got it?' he queried.

Luke shook his head.

Now Geis gave Ingels a straightforward look that was tinged with something unspoken. He breathed, 'That's fine! Don't you see it, Sam!'

'See what?'

'He ain't been wearin' his badge. No one knows he works for us!' Geis caught himself and added hastily, 'For you.'

Ingels looked at Luke and began hotly, 'Either you wear that badge or ...'

'Wear it, nothin'!' the saloon-owner cut in. 'Luke, I've got a job for you.'

Luke nodded. 'I was beginnin' to wonder what I was drawin' my pay for.'

'Here it is.' ... Geis leaned forward in his chair, speaking intently ... 'This Luke Barron, or whoever's operatin' under his name, has got this town spooked. It's so bad the claim-owners are poolin' their gold and keepin' it under guard. When they get enough for a shipment, they're goin' to try and run it through on their own, probably at night. Now I've got a hunch that it's some of their own tribe that have been doing the night-riding. Here's Sam, the law, and he's got half a dozen good deputies. Do they come to him for protection? Will they come to him for a guard when they ship that gold out?

'No! Instead of trustin' the law, they suspect Sam of havin' a hand in this Luke Barron scare. They even suspect me!'

'You don't say,' Luke drawled, smiling faintly.

Geis saw that Luke was catching on. He went on, poker-faced, with a proper show of indignation: 'So what're we to do? Let those poor jaspers lose their shirts when it comes to shippin' their gold out? Let this Luke Barron's bunch hi-jack the gold stage and help themselves? Hell, no! We're goin' to give that stage the protection it needs. Even though the claim-owners won't know it, we're sending our own guards along to see that the gold gets out safely. In the process, we'll probably have the chance to trap this Luke Barron outfit and blow it to doll rags! When the claim-owners see what we've done for 'em, maybe they'll give us a regular contract to take their gold out. That's where your bonus comes in.'

Sam Ingels was staring at the *Nugget* owner with wide-open incredulous eyes. But Geis wasn't looking at him as Luke drawled, 'What's my job?'

'Don't you get it? You haven't worn your badge. No one knows you're a deputy sheriff. We can send you up to mosey 'round the diggin's and pick up information for us.'

'Such as when the gold shipment is to be made?'

'When it's to be made, how much is going out, how many guards are being sent along.'

Ingels breathed, 'Matt, that's the best idea you've had in a month! Wipe out that wild bunch and this town can start sleepin' nights again.' The lawman even went so far as to wink slyly at Geis, thinking he wasn't observed. But Luke caught that wink and filed it at the back of his mind as one more tangible crumb of proof that Matt Geis and Sam Ingels were guiltier than half the men named on the reward notices in the file in the sheriff's office.

Geis said, 'Another thing. While you're prowlin' around up there, see if you can pick up any sign on this jail-break last night. There's a gent up there by the name of Randall, George Randall. He's an old bird that likes the bottle. Take a bottle along and offer him a drink. Get him to talking and you may get all the information we want right there.' ... He leaned back in the swivel-chair, rubbing his palms together ... 'This is beginning to shape up real nice. What'd I tell you, Sam? We can use Luke. And that business out front about saving the old woman her two pails of water may come in handy. Anyone who gets away with anything against me is a friend of those rannies up at the diggin's whether he wants to be or not!'

SIX

Later, as Luke came into the foot of the diggin's, riding his grey, Matt Geis's words were proved correct. Whether it was yesterday's run-in with Sam Ingels or today's incident of saving the old woman her two pails of water at Matt Geis's well, Luke couldn't tell; but the fact remained that he was made welcome at the diggin's.

Almost the first man that laid eyes on him, grubbing in the sand along the canyon-bottom with pick, pan and shovel, straightened, looked at him sharply, then called cordially, 'Mornin', stranger! We was hopin' you'd be up here. Ma Baker told us all about it.'

'About what?' Luke queried, reining the grey to a stand.

'You buckin' the house man down there at the *Nugget* a while ago. Say! How come you're packin' an iron?' As had happened yesterday when he stopped the girl in front of the saloon, this man's eyes had gone to Luke's gun and remained fastened on it.

'No one's tried to make me hide it,' Luke answered.

The claim-owner slapped his knee and guffawed at the reply. He hailed his closest neighbor fifty yards up the draw and presently a dozen or more men had gathered around him and were talking eagerly to Luke. What had Matt Geis said yesterday after the kick in the guts he'd given Sam Ingels? Had Ingels tried to arrest him? What had happened this morning after he'd given the old woman the two pails of water?

Luke debated his answers carefully. They'd let him keep his guns providing he didn't cause trouble. Sam Ingels had tried to hire him as a deputy and been turned down. Geis had warned him a second time this morning, after the incident of the water.

'You mean to say you got them two buffaloed?' one claim-owner asked incredulously. Then, eagerly: 'What do you aim to do from now on?'

'Look for work,' Luke answered. 'I understand George Randall's got something in mind for me.'

At first a few laughs greeted his answer. Then, mysteriously, the men agreed that it would be a good thing for him to call on George Randall. One even came out openly and said, 'If Randall's thinkin' of gathering a pack to go against Geis, he can call on me!' Several others agreed with him.

Lifting his hand as he left them, Luke went on

soberly considering these evidences of men who had, until now, worked and eaten and slept haunted by a fear for their lives and the scant ounces of yellow dust they were taking from the placers. These men were an assortment of all breeds, some honest, some obviously not; but all were drawn together by one common denominator, fear, and all reached out eagerly for the help of a man who would show them a way out from under the threat of the past weeks. They thought that he, Luke, was to be that man.

Climbing on up the canyon, he saw evidence of the enormous amount of work these men had put in to make their claims workable. Water was at a premium. To conserve it, a common sluice had been built along the east wall flanking the diggin's. Guards carrying clubs patrolled the sluice, seeing that each man took no more than his share of water. The bed of the canyon was torn up into hundreds of holes, piles of pay-dirt and, higher beyond the sluice, discarded tailings that had been worked for gold. Crude shacks were unevenly spaced along the near-wall. The further Luke rode, the more activity there was on the claims. Above, a good number of them were fenced strongly with barbed wire. They became bigger, too, worked by more men, and ore-wagons that hauled the pay-dirt down out of the hills. Finally, at the furthest point, a strong six-wire fence enclosed the biggest claim of all.

At a narrow gate in this fence was a boldly-lettered sign. *Keep out! Trespassers Enter at Their Own Risk! Matthew Geis, Owner.*

Here, then, were the claims, the mother lode, that Matt Geis had won from George Randall in that fatal game of cards that ended with Geis the owner of the richest part of the diggin's, with Randall a poor and almost penniless man. Upwards of thirty men worked the sands along the creek bottom inside Geis's fence. In there, opposite, the sluice started from a pool where the scant waters of the creek had been dammed. The workers in there seemed to have no regard for waste of water, spilling it from sluiceboxes and rockers with a carelessness that was symbolic of the iron grip of authority Matt Geis held on this boom-camp. And here Luke saw guns, many guns, where below he hadn't spotted one. This claim was well guarded. From the stony glances given him by two men guarding the gate, Luke knew that those guns would be used if the occasion arose.

'Any idea where I can find George Randall?' he inquired of the pair.

Instead of answering his question, one of them asked gruffly: 'Where'd you get the iron?'

Luke produced his deputy's badge readily enough, eager to get on to Randall's where Ed waited, not particularly caring about putting these two gunnies in their place. His show of the badge produced immediate results. 'On up there around the bend,' he was told, and rode on.

Randall's shack was different from those he had seen below, even though it was built of the same material as most, raw lumber, lath and tarpaper. Its outline was the same as the others, low, squat and flat-roofed. But it stood on a low knoll beside the narrow stream and flowers grew at either side of its doorway. A tall cedar, the first of many that grew along the canyon above this point, shaded it coolly from the sun's pitiless glare. In the two windows that faced down-canyon were curtains; these and the garden were visible evidence of a woman's hand that had been lacking in the ugly littered yards around the shacks down-canyon. This dwelling had the look of permanency, of a home.

As Luke rode up the knoll, the door opened and a man stepped out of it. He was well beyond middle age and wore a close-clipped grey beard that didn't quite hide the sharp angles of a hawkish face. His frame, stooped slightly at the shoulders, was spare. A long acquaintance with the sun had blackened his face and at the corners of the eye-sockets were webbed lines that further marked him for what he was, a grizzled old prospector who had spent many seasons staring into the bright glare of the desert's hot sands.

'George Randall?' Luke queried, as he reined in a few feet out from the door.

'That's me,' Randall answered briefly. His lack of an invitation for Luke to dismount made plain the look in his eyes, which was faintly hostile. It was obvious that George Randall thought himself a friendless man.

Luke took the most direct way that occurred to him of wiping out the old prospector's wariness. 'Ed Tyler here?'

Randall's look sharpened, turning even more wary. 'Who's Tyler?'

'He told me when he left me last night he was headed for here.'

Suddenly Randall's manner changed.

He even smiled meagrely as he drawled, 'You must be him, Luke, the one Ed mentioned. Only we wasn't lookin' for you until after dark. Light down, won't you?' He turned and called, 'It's all right, Nan. You can come out. And bring a dipper of water with you. I've got a thirsty man out here.'

Inside, Luke heard the ring of a dipper against a tin pail. As he swung aground, he asked, 'Where's Ed?'

Randall jerked his head toward the abrupt slope of the near canyon wall. 'Up there somewheres. Said he wouldn't run us the risk of stayin' at the house. So we give him a blanket, some grub and a jug of water last night. He's due down right after dark.'

As the oldster finished speaking, a figure moved out the doorway behind him. Luke gave a start of sheer surprise as he recognized the girl he'd yesterday talked to in front of the *Nugget*, the girl who had yesterday worn a man's outfit and who was today utterly feminine in a tight-waisted dress of calico print. Her ash-blonde hair was now a mass of white gold bound tightly over her head by two braids gathered at the nape of a slender shapely neck. Yesterday he had thought her pretty. Today she was beautiful.

SEVEN

Nancy Randall handed her father the dipper of water. He passed it across to Luke. 'Nancy, this is Ed's friend, Luke.' ... He gave a laugh ... 'Ed told us about Geis givin' you your new handle.'

Luke accepted the drink, taking his glance from the girl. He was aware that whatever Ed had told these two had accomplished its purpose. Randall was showing range courtesy in not being curious about his real name. He was also accepting him as his friend.

'How come you rode up here in broad daylight?' Randall queried.

Luke told him of the errand Geis had sent him on, and while he talked the sober expression of a moment ago gathered again on the prospector's face. When he had finished, Randall said worriedly: 'We didn't look for anyone to find out about the gold. Well, it's done now and we'll have to think of something else. There ain't a lot a man can be certain of these days. Take even Ed Tyler.

When I asked him why you and him was slingin' in with us, he said you had your own reasons, that he wanted to even things with the law. I reckon I can be satisfied with that, so long as you're helpin' us. But what'll the others say when it comes to trustin' you?'

Luke had the impulse to admit the truth, who he was, that he had come here to clear his name. But a look at Nancy Randall stifled the impulse, for he was thinking that admitting he was an outlaw would lessen her respect for him. Strangely enough, he was concerned at what this girl might think of him.

But he could tell half the truth and now he said, 'Maybe you had a look at that reward-notice the sheriff showed the mob the other day when they put Ed up for trial. Ed sided Luke across in Colorado. And he knows that Barron has a pardon from the governor of Texas and headed back there a month ago. So it can't be Barron on the loose up here and Ed wants to put that straight. As for me, I've known Ed for ten years. When I heard he was in trouble, I came up to get him out of it. One thing led to another and here we are. It was Ed who decided to stay on and help put down this Luke scare. Guess he wants to clear Barron's name, since he knows his old partner isn't behind these shenanigans.'

Randall listened in frowning concentration. Luke's explanation seemed to satisfy him, for he said, 'That sounds likely. Why didn't Ed put it to me that way 'stead of hedgin' like he did last night?'

'Ed's pretty close-mouthed,' Luke said casually. 'You never know what's goin' on inside that head of his. But about this other, this gold that's bein' shipped out. It …'

'It ain't goin' to be shipped out now! Not so long as Geis knows about it.'

'I've got an idea it should be shipped. The sooner the better,' Luke told him. 'Only not the way Geis thinks. Get your stage ready. Instead of fillin' your money-chest with dust, fill it with sand. Load the stage to the axles with guards. Then …'

'But we ain't got any guns! They're all checked down there at the cottonwood and those damn deputies would not let us have 'em for love nor money if they knew why we wanted 'em. We were countin' on sneaking the stage down the road at night.'

'You can get guns. Any man leaving the lower town limits has a right to his gun. Have your guards go down the trail the day before the stage leaves, say tomorrow. They hide their guns below somewhere. Then, the day after, load your stage with that chestful of sand and pile your guards on and leave town. Pick the guns up down the canyon.'

'If the gold ain't in the stage, what's the use of runnin' that kind of a sandy?'

'To decoy the bunch that's after the gold. They'll stop the stage somewhere along the trail out. Your guards can high-tail and leave the stage, take to the brush.' He paused a moment, remembering something he had noticed riding in. 'There's a side road forks from the main trail right below town, isn't there?'

Randall nodded, puzzled at what Luke was driving at. 'Leads down into Rattler Canyon. It's rough and washed out but a man can get through. Hits the main trail out beyond the hills.'

'Then send a man in a light rig on down ahead of the stage. Send him alone. Load the rig with whatever you want, maybe furniture, like it was a man headed out for good. Pack the gold in with the load. Have your man take the trail through Rattler Canyon to be sure nothing goes wrong. Before anyone knows what's happened, your gold's in the bank below.'

Randall's eyes sparkled with ready admiration. Luke was more interested in the girl's reaction, which was like her father's. Randall hit an open palm with clenched fist. 'It'll work! Slick as saddlesoap. Won't it, Nan?'

As the prospector turned to his daughter, Luke had a brief insight into how greatly the father depended on the daughter's judgment. If he hadn't known what lay behind it, Luke would have seen it as a sign of weakness in Randall, for men rarely asked a woman's opinion on such a vital point as this. But Luke knew Randall's history, or part of it, mainly the fact that this girl had recently saved her father from drinking himself into oblivion. It was obvious that Randall depended on her judgment now and that quality in him was to be more admired than disrespected.

'I ... I hope no one will be hurt,' the girl said in a low voice. Looking at Luke with a strange light in her eyes, she said abruptly: 'You're the one to take the gold out!'

'I am?'

She nodded. 'In case anything goes wrong, you'll know what to do. It will be like ... like your breaking in the roof of the jail last night to get Ed Tyler out. No one would have thought of that. But you did.'

As she paid him this high compliment, Nancy Randall's face colored a little. But more important than that was her look that beseeched him to do as she asked.

She must have seen him wavering before her impulsive request, for she added quickly: 'You don't know how bad things are here. There isn't a man here who will trust his neighbor these days. If one was named to drive the gold down Rattler, someone would object. No two would agree.'

'Why should they trust me?'

'They will trust you,' the girl told him gravely. 'I know. You have that look about you. And they'll remember what you did yesterday to Sam Ingels.'

Randall put it, 'She's right, Luke! You're the man to do it.'

'What excuse can I have for driving a rig out of town?'

The oldster's mind had been at work these past moments as his daughter urged Luke to help them. Now he had a ready answer to Luke's question: 'Everyone knows Nan doesn't like these diggin's. Everyone knows she's been tryin' to get me to leave. Suppose I load most of the stuff from the shack into a buckboard? Suppose I let it get around that you've fallen for Nan and she's asked you to help us move out? Then ...'

'Dad!' the girl protested.

'Why not?' Randall asked, looking at her levelly. 'We'll only be pretendin'. Luke can get that gold down and bring our stuff back again. He can make the whole trip in a day.'

'I'll let you say those things about me if you really will leave,' Nan said, in proof of her genuine feeling of wanting to put this dark chapter of her father's life in these diggin's forever in the past.

But Randall stubbornly shook his head. 'I was the first man in here. Me and two pack-burros. I'll be the last to leave. Heck, Nan, why leave when we've found a way of fightin' Matt Geis, when we've found a man to boss things like they should be?'

Luke could see the hope die out of the girl's eyes, then the real anger that came into them.

But for the interruption that came at this moment, the whistle that sounded from the patch of scrub cedar up the hill-slope close by, he didn't know what might have happened to destroy the momentarily thin surface of harmony between the prospector and his daughter.

At the sound of that call all three turned to look above. There, waving down to them from the concealment of a cedar, was Ed Tyler.

Randall gave a quick glance down-canyon. He said sharply, 'Stay here, Nan! Give us a call if anyone comes up the trail.' He led the way up the slope, Luke following.

Ed Tyler's dark homely face took on a broad grin as Luke walked up to him. 'You've got gall, strayin' up here at this time o' day!'

They talked a minute or so, Randall and Luke posting Ed on recent developments and the plan for taking the gold out.

Ed agreed to everything but had something to add: 'George, you know we've thought all along that this wild bunch was forted up someplace in the canyon? Well, last night I couldn't sleep, being slept out from them two weeks in jail. I was sittin' up on the rim, wide awake, about two this mornin' when I happened to see a jasper ridin' up that way. Thinks I, why prowl around this time of the night, mister? So I followed him. I found that camp. It's in a box-canyon less'n three miles from here.'

'How many men?' Luke asked as Randall swore excitedly.

'Couldn't tell exactly. They've thrown up a pole cabin and there's good pasture for their cayuses. I counted four around the fire at breakfast. There may have been more sleepin' late. There's a trail down off the rim, too, a plenty steep one. They must use both ways into the place.'

'Geis's men?' This from Randall.

Ed nodded. 'I saw Shorty Taylor and Mart Kemp. The other two I didn't know.'

'This may come in handy later,' Luke said.

'Why later? Why not take a few rifles up there tonight and let 'em taste some lead?'

Luke considered this. At first he was against the idea. But on second thought, to raid Geis's camp might help by letting the saloon-owner know he wasn't having things all his own way. If the raid was convincing enough, Geis might even abandon his move to raid the gold stage.

So Luke said, 'All right, Randall can get some men to side you. But get men you can trust. Ten to one, Geis has understrappers planted through the diggin's who'll tip him off to what's up if you spread the news too far.'

'Just what I was thinkin' about shippin' that gold out,' Randall said. 'No one's to know you're takin' it down Rattler, Luke. No one but the four or five men we pick as guards, and ourselves.'

'So long as this play is comin' off tonight,

tomorrow would be a good time to take the gold out,' Luke said.

'Yeah, before they get time to get organized again,' Ed agreed.

'You have to pick your men today then,' Luke said. 'And send them down to cache their guns. Can you arrange things, lettin' your men know the gold is ready to go out, hiring the stage on such short notice?'

'It won't be me that does it. Frank Summers is head man of the diggin's. But he'll work along with us.'

'Then I can tell Geis the gold goes out tomorrow?'

Randall nodded.

Ed said, 'Gents, this thing's shapin' up right nice!' He all at once held out his hand. 'Got the makin's, Luke? I smoked mine all up last night.'

Luke took a Durham-sack from his shirt and passed it across.

EIGHT

From behind a high rock outcropping at the bend of the canyon directly below George Randall's shack, the man holding the reins of a roan horse saw Luke hand across his tobacco to someone standing in the concealment of the stunted cedar up the slope. For the past quarter-hour, this watcher had made careful note of Luke's every move, since Matt Geis had sent him on that particular errand.

Until a few moments ago, the *Nugget* man had been very uninterested in his job. Matt Geis had told him that the new deputy was headed for George Randall's, had directed him to follow leisurely and observe the tall stranger's actions. He had seen Luke ride up to the cabin, meet Randall and then the girl and stand talking for long minutes. Then had come the whistle from the hill.

The whistle aroused the curiosity of the watcher at the bend. When Luke and Randall went up to the clump of cedar and stood talking, well out of earshot, his curiosity became even stronger. And now the passing across of that sack of tobacco was the first evidence he had that Luke and Randall had gone up there to talk to someone who took the pains to stay hidden behind the scrubby tree.

Five minutes later, Luke and Randall came back down the slope. Luke talked a moment with the girl, then swung into the hull of his grey horse. The man at the bend quickly left his post, mounted the roan, and rode back down the canyon keeping to the sandy creek-bottom so that the sound of his going would be muffled.

He wasted no time returning to town and the *Nugget*, little more in telling Matt Geis what he had seen and heard. Listening, the saloon-owner stiffened from a slouch to a stiff uprightness in his chair behind the mahogany desk. A careful man, he had sent this man to follow Luke only out of habit of watching every new man closely for the first few days.

'Go find Sam Ingels and send him here!' he snapped when he had heard the story. 'Hurry about it! Then come back here and wait at the bar until I send for you. Tell Hod your drinks are on the house.'

Ingels was a long time in appearing. While he waited, Geis got up from the desk and paced the floor of his office restlessly, his eyes smouldering in dark anger. By the time the tread of the sheriff's boots approached the office door, he was regretting the impulse that had made him send for the lawman. Ingels was of little use when it came to a thing like this, so little, in fact, that by the time the door opened Geis had decided to keep what he knew to himself.

'Want me?' Ingels said upon entering the room.

'Yeah. Thought you ought to be here when Luke gets back. He's on his way in now. I sent Gonzales out to watch him. Want to wait here or outside?'

'I could stand a drink,' Ingels said, and sauntered back out.

Alone again, Geis started pacing the floor once more. He didn't stop to ask himself why he was letting this stranger worry him, knowing only that he was being betrayed by this new deputy whose arrogance and quickness with a gun had seemed to make him an ideal man to hire. Randall and this stranger had gone up the hill above Randall's shack to talk with someone who was careful not to expose himself. That someone was probably Ed Tyler, Luke Barron's lieutenant.

'Luke Barron!'

Geis breathed the name aloud, suddenly stopping in his tracks. 'And, by God, he had the nerve to admit it!'

In that brief moment of keen insight, Matt Geis's shrewdness came to his aid. With the meagre tell-tale signs picked up by the man he had sent to follow the stranger, he had suddenly arrived at a startling conclusion. This new deputy could be Luke Barron! He was Luke Barron! Hadn't he said that was his name?

Geis swore softly when he remembered passing the stranger's statement off as a joke. Wasn't it reasonable to suppose that Ed Tyler might have had a chance to get the word out about the things that were going on here before he was arrested that night after his first appearance in Bonanza? Wasn't it logical that he should have immediately written Luke Barron, telling of the game that was being played under cover of his name?

Geis's booming laugh suddenly echoed into the room. He was feeling better now. He liked nothing better than playing a hand like this, with marked cards where he knew exactly what his opponent held against him. 'So this jasper's Barron himself, eh?' he drawled under his breath, and laughed again.

He lit a cigar, smoking it furiously. By the time the knock sounded at his door the room was blue with smoke. But by that time he knew what he was going to do.

He answered the knock and Luke and Ingels entered.

'Any luck?' he asked, seating himself at the desk.

'Some.' Luke took the time to finish rolling a smoke before he went on: 'You didn't send me up there any too soon. And you were right about the welcome they'd hand me. Randall talked. The gold goes out tomorrow mornin'.'

Ingels said, 'That's risky, ain't it? I'd think they'd try and sneak it through at night.'

'Randall says not. They decided they might get the help of whoever's on the road if they run into trouble. They're counting on pickin' up a few guns at the cottonwood on the way out.'

Geis smiled. 'Sam, your man'll have to file off a few firin'-pins before tomorrow, won't he? What else did you pick up, Luke?'

'Not much. Randall's leavin' town for good, right after his stage pulls out. He's hired a buckboard to haul his stuff down. I'm drivin' it down for him.'

'*You* are?' Geis was obviously surprised, not at the news of Randall's departure, which had been rumoured these last few days, but at Luke's last statement. 'How come?'

Luke shrugged. 'They needed help. I offered.'

All at once Geis thought he understood what lay behind this new development. 'That girl of his been usin' her eyes again?' Catching the flush that came to Luke's face, his laugh came, raucously. 'Who'd have thought you'd fall for a skirt, Luke!'

'Careful, Geis!' Luke's flat drawl carried a note of warning.

'Hell, I didn't mean nothin'! Forget it. Put your halter on that filly and you've got the pick of any string. But how you figure to court her if she's leavin'?'

At first, Luke resented the coarse inference behind the saloon-owner's words and laugh. But now Geis had quickly changed his manner to one that lacked all offense. Luke had nearly lost his temper but had it in check again. 'They're settlin' down in town below,' he answered. 'Thirty miles isn't a far ride any day work slacks off here.'

'Let's go out and have a drink on it!' Geis offered in hearty affability. And on the way to the bar, he added, 'You did a nice job. Stick with me, and I'll see you're taken care of.'

NINE

The rest of that day and early evening saw Luke restless and on edge. Without being able to define why, he sensed that something was wrong. Having little acquaintance with Matt Geis, he didn't trust his hunch that Geis's affability this morning had been a sham, that the saloon-owner was hiding some knowledge that didn't quite tally with his actions. But even though he was unwilling to trust that hunch, it turned him unconsciously wary. Loafing at the *Nugget*'s bar two hours after eating his evening meal, he took care to stand at the front end of the counter with his back to the wall. Before eating, he'd joined a desultory, low-stake game of draw poker; and then, too, he'd been careful to put a wall behind his chair.

The *Nugget* was crowded now, three barkeeps working at top speed, the beat of the piano and the couples on the dance-floor at the rear making a lesser din than the coarse laughter and voices of

the men around the gambling tables and those
doing the drinking. The air was foul with the reek
of stale beer, whiskey and tobacco-smoke. Luke
wanted to leave the place yet didn't, expecting
developments.

They came shortly after ten o'clock, with the
appearance of a man Luke recognized as the
deputy who had this morning been stationed at
the water-valve of Geis's well in front of the
saloon.

The deputy came through the swing doors in a
hurry, his right hand clenched about his left
forearm, the sleeve of which was stained darkly
with blood. His face was pale, yellow instead of
bronze, and his Stetson was pushed onto the back
of his head to show his forehead beady with
perspiration.

He pushed on back through the crowd, making
for Geis's office. He ignored the greetings of
several acquaintances on the way. After his
disappearance into the office, a momentary lull
that had greeted his appearance held on a
moment or two and finally faded. Luke called for
his third glass of bourbon and in the five minute
interval that followed didn't touch the liquor.

The office door swung open again, and Geis, in
shirt-sleeves, stood framed in it. He motioned to
three men at the far end of the bar and they went
across to him. He spoke to them, then disappeared
a moment and returned wearing his coat.

He and his trio of men, all wearing guns, moved back through the crowd toward the front. He spotted Luke and swung aside from his men.

'Want to come along?' he asked, and the look in his eye was flinty.

'Where to?'

'The diggin's. We're goin' through it with a fine-tooth comb ... for guns.'

'Didn't know they were allowed up the canyon.'

'They ain't!' the *Nugget* owner spoke tersely. 'Comin'?'

'Sure.'

Luke followed him out to the walk, where they were joined by the three others. On the way across to the stage-barn for their horses, Geis announced briefly: 'Bunch of my men camped up the canyon got shot up tonight.'

'Bad?'

The muscles on the saloon-owner's jowled face stood out sharply. He nodded. 'Two cashed in, three others may later.'

Luke's face was inscrutable. 'Why were they campin' up there?'

Geis smiled thinly, lied. 'Trying to save on expense money. It costs plenty to live in town. A bunch of 'em slung in together, threw up a shack and hung out up there.'

Luke kept his face straight. He knew and Geis knew that he knew this wasn't the truth. He queried: 'Why look in the diggin's for the men that did it?'

'Who else could it be but Randall and his friends? They're the only bunch around here that hates my guts bad enough to make a play like this.'

'Randall seemed mild enough today.'

'He'll fool you. He made the original strike here, staked out the first claims. Then, one night down below where I ran a saloon before I came here, he got stinkin' drunk and lost his claims at one of my poker layouts. Now he holds the grudge against me.'

That was the end of the talking. They saddled at the barn and headed quickly up the muddy street, their horses slogging for the diggin's. Beyond the upper town, in the stretch where tents marked the lower limits of the staked ground, Geis called a halt and told his men: 'We'll begin with Frank Summers. Sid, you and Marty go in alone. If Summers is there, push him around! If he ain't warn the old woman off the place, search his shack for a gun and then fire the damn' thing. Harv, you go on to Bill Mathers and do the same. Get a move on!'

He motioned Luke to remain with him as his men left. 'We'll coast along easy and let 'em get started.'

'You're pretty sure about this, Geis.'

The *Nugget* man laughed softly. 'I've been sure for a long time. Maybe tomorrow they'll feel more like takin' my price.'

'Price for what?'

'Their claims. I've offered to buy any or all of 'em out, for a fair price. So far they haven't listened. Maybe they will now.' ... He paused a brief moment, thinking of something, looking at Luke ... 'Come to think of it, we can pay a call ourselves.'

'George Randall?'

Geis shook his head. 'No use botherin' with that old souse. He's leaving tomorrow anyway, which suits me. I'm thinking of Doc Savage.'

Remembering Ed's mention of the doctor's efforts to loosen Geis's hold on Bonanza's only supply of good water, Luke nevertheless asked blandly: 'Friend of yours?'

'No, by God! But I have a hankerin' to know what he's been up to the last two or three hours.'

Doc Savage's makeshift hospital was a plain tarpaper shack that squatted on a wide rock shelf at the foot of the sheer east wall a few hundred yards beyond the first down-canyon tent. A light shone through two front windows. Geis remarked acidly, 'Up past his bed time,' and a moment later reached out suddenly to take Luke by the arm and signal a halt.

They were coming up obliquely on the shack, in sight of its rear corner. Geis pointed back there where two horses stood tied in the heavy shadows close in to the canyon wall outlined against the grey shape of a tent. 'See the paint horse? He's Fred Jeliff's! Fred's one more jasper we're goin' to invite to leave tonight. Know what his bein' here means?'

Luke shook his head.

'Come along. I'll show you!'

There was something in Geis's tone that warned Luke of the man's cool anger as they rode in to the front of the hospital, came aground and tied their horses.

At Geis's knock on the door, it opened. Nancy Randall stood there, wearing a white apron and with a white nurse's cap pinned high on her blonde head.

Geis was courteous, tipping his hat and pretending not to notice the look of alarm that crossed the girl's face: 'Savage in?' he asked politely.

The girl didn't answer at once, seeing Luke now for the first time. His being here with Geis seemed to reassure her a little, for the paleness of a moment ago left her face. She shook her head and was about to speak when Geis said: 'That's him back there, ain't it?' When he mounted the last step, about to enter the door, there was nothing she could do but move aside.

Bonanza's hospital consisted of a single long room and a curtained side alcove that Luke supposed served as a combination office and operating room. Half a dozen cots lined each side wall. Five of the cots were occupied. In front of the curtain that hid the alcove stood a man Luke

knew must be Savage. He wore a white coat and a
stethoscope hung from his neck.

What took Luke's instant attention was the
hardening of Savage's blocky honest face at sight
of Matt Geis. The brown eyes that Luke decided
could be kindly and warm took on a flinty look of
anger. Savage was short-statured and heavy.
There was about him a look of competence and a
strong willfulness.

Geis drawled smoothly, 'Evenin', Doc. Am I
buttin' in on somethin'?'

Luke caught the swift, almost furtive, look
Savage directed toward the curtain of the alcove.
Then the doctor moved quickly away from the
curtain, saying, 'Nothing that won't wait. Miss
Randall was here helping me clear out my office.'

Geis gave a deprecatory wave of the hand.
'Don't mind that! Let's go in and sit. There's
something I wanted to talk over with you.'

He started toward the curtain. Savage's
reaction was immediate. He reached out and took
Geis by the arm, guiding him toward an empty
cot. 'The floor's wet in there,' he said hastily, a
little uncertainly. 'Been mopping it up. We can
talk here.'

Matt Geis suddenly reached out and swept the
curtain aside. In the small cubby-hole, fitted with
a white padded wooden table, a desk, two white
cabinets, were two men. One lay on the table,
upper body naked, the stain of blood on the white

skin over his ribs along his side. His eyes were closed. The other, rising up off the edge of the desk, caught so much by surprise that he instinctively reached for the holstered gun at his thigh, had his left arm in a sling.

Matt Geis's right hand made a two-inch move upward toward the shoulder-holster beneath his coat, then settled back along his side. He ignored the gun that nosed up at him from the thigh of the man with the bad arm. An ugly grimace crossed his face.

Swinging around slowly on Savage, he drawled, 'This about finishes your stay here, Doc.'

The two patients were obviously claim-owners who had been wounded in the raid on the camp up the canyon led by Ed Tyler and George Randall tonight.

Savage's anger cut loose with a directness that surprised even Luke: 'Get out, Geis! Get out before you're thrown out!'

Geis smiled now, his look taking in the girl who stood close beside Luke. Nancy Randall's face had gone pale once more; there was more anger than fear in her eyes, though, and it was clear to Luke that if a man was ever the target of outright hate, Matt Geis was that target at this moment.

'I'll go,' Geis breathed. 'But I'll be back, Savage! Unless you've cleared this camp by this time tomorrow.'

'Want me to let this thing off, Doc?' calmly

drawled the wounded man who held the gun lined at Geis. Two patients had elbowed up on their cots and were witnessing this.

TEN

Savage made no reply and Luke couldn't be sure that the medico had heard the question, so intent was the look he fixed on the saloon-owner. 'I'm staying, Geis,' he stated levelly. 'Staying whether or not you like it! These men were badly hurt tonight. It doesn't matter whose bullets they stopped. They're in need of my care. Anyone can come here and ask that of me.'

'Why aren't you up the canyon patchin' up my men?' All pretense had left Geis now, his admission that men in his pay had been in the camp up the canyon coming without hesitation.

'Because these two brought me the first word I had of the fight. When I finish with them, I intend going up there to help the others.'

Geis shook his head, his sneer deepening. 'I reckon we're not that hard up.'

'Suit yourself. While we're talking on it, there's a man with typhoid in a tent out back. He'll be the first of many. He has typhoid because he couldn't afford to buy your water, Geis! Because he's too poor to even buy decent food!'

'I dug that well! I didn't keep the town council from diggin' another! If these jaspers are fools enough to get into a spot like this, let 'em take their medicine.'

'That's another thing. We're shy on medicine, Geis. Terribly shy! If someone doesn't donate some money to buy what's necessary to control things, Bonanza's going to have an epidemic on its hands. Your saloon, every public gathering place in town, will be closed under quarantine!'

Geis's expression sobered. 'You're sure about that?'

Savage nodded, his stare still flinty. 'Dead sure. It's my duty to report a typhoid case to the county authorities.'

The big man's hand went into his pocket. He brought out a wallet, unfolded it and thumbed out several bills. 'How much?'

'Nothing … from you, Geis!'

'Hell, you just finished sayin' you were short of funds!'

'We are. But we'll get the money somehow. That's blood-money you've got, money you charged for rotten liquor, for water you should be giving away. I don't need money that badly.'

Geis tossed the bills across onto the cot. The man with the gun in the alcove said, 'You heard what he said! He don't want it! Pick it up, stuff it in your pocket and be on your way! *Pronto!*'

The feverish half-mad gleam in the wounded man's eyes warned Luke, even if it didn't Geis. Luke drawled, 'Better do as he says, Geis.'

Only at his smooth-drawled words did Geis's reasoning return. He stooped over and took the money from the cot. He followed Luke to the door, throwing the panel back against the wall. Pausing there while Luke went out ahead of him, he turned back toward the alcove: 'Parsons, you and Jeliff better be a hell of a long ways from here by sun-up.'

Out front, Luke heard the jarring explosion of the gun, saw the bullet knock a chip from the door-frame not two inches from Geis's elbow. The *Nugget* owner made an ungraceful lunge out the door, wheeling in behind the wall. His hand flicked upwards, arching out a stubby-barreled .45.

Luke reached out and pushed his arm down. 'Better wait for a better chance, Geis. They're primed for you this time.'

Geis jerked his arm away and turned on Luke, hot rage showing on his shadowed face. Then that look clouded over before a return of level-headed shrewdness. He even laughed softly as he thrust the gun back in under his coat. 'Come along,' he said, 'we'll take care of those two!'

They were crossing the plank bridge over the sluice, Geis leading the way at a fast trot, when he slowed enough to let Luke close in on him and said, 'The boys didn't waste much time.' He pointed up-canyon, toward the rosy glow of two fires that reddened the night up there.

'Looks like they'd had some practice,' Luke drawled, and his lean face didn't mirror the amusement of Geis's answering chuckle.

The *Nugget* owner led the way back to town with his gelding at a run, cursing as the jam of traffic in the upper street slowed them for a moment. Luke, thinking back on his second meeting with Nan Randall, was wondering what lay behind Geis's threatening statement as they left the hospital and his apparent hurry to get back to town.

He found out when they were still fifty yards short of the *Nugget*'s crowded entrance. Geis spotted the sheriff crossing the street and hailed him, riding up on the lawman just out from the tie rail opposite the saloon.

Geis leaned down in the saddle and told Ingels crisply, 'Bad news, Sam. A bunch of diggin's men shot up the camp tonight. They ...'

'I heard about it,' Ingels cut in. 'Was just out lookin' for you.'

'Luke and I went to the hospital on the hunch Savage might have had some patchin' to do. We found Parsons and Jeliff there getting doctored for lead poisonin'. Jeliff pulled a gun on me and we had to leave. I want you to get a man and go up there and arrest 'em both. Take Ramirez or Kemp. Hold 'em for murder.'

'What's the matter with Luke here?'

Geis hesitated for a moment longer than was necessary. Luke knew instantly that his hunch earlier tonight had been correct. Geis knew something about him, didn't trust him.

But the saloon-owner covered his indecision nicely the next moment: 'All right, take Luke, Parsons was hurt bad, probably can't be moved. Let him go while you get Jeliff. Go to Jeliff's tent first. If he makes a stray move, let him have it!' ... He swung down out of the saddle.... 'You can take my jughead. Make it fast!'

Stepping into the saddle, Ingels said worriedly, 'I hope to hell you know what you're doin', Matt! Prod those jaspers hard enough, and we'll have 'em swarmin' down on us!'

'The sooner the better,' Geis stated. 'When they do, we'll be ready.'

ELEVEN

At a narrowing in the canyon close above the
hospital Ingels drew rein and motioned Luke to
stop. He pointed ahead and to the left. 'Jeliff's
tent's off there, up the slope a ways. You work
around behind and cover it from the back. I'll give
you a minute to get set.'

Luke queried: 'What if he isn't alone?'

'What if he ain't? I'm goin' straight in and hail.
If they throw down on me, you'll have 'em where I
want 'em. There's room in the jail for as many as
want to come.'

Luke swung aside, turning left. The grey
slogged up a loose drift of talus, gained a rocky
shoulder and travelled a level open stretch of rock.
Off to his right, Luke could see the pale blob of
Jeliff's tent against the night's obscurity, judging
it to be fifty or sixty yards away. Momentarily, he
didn't know what he was going to do. Then on
sudden impulse he came aground, dropped the
grey's reins and started toward Jeliff's tent at a
run.

Coming up on it, he called softly, 'Jeliff!' listening, hoping to be warned of the sheriff's approach before it was too late.

He had no answer and hesitated only a moment before stepping up to the tent, unlacing the flap and stepping in. By the light of a match cupped in his hand, he took a brief glimpse of the inside. There was a cot, a pile of dunnage in one corner and a crate packed with tinned food. From behind it, he saw the barrel-end of a rifle.

He heard the hoof-strike of Ingels' gelding climbing the slope as he reached for the rifle. It was a carbine, a Winchester. It was loaded.

He raised the back drop of the tent and crawled out, running as soundlessly as he could toward a patch of stunted cedar a bare twenty yards away and to the left, toward his horse. He swung in behind the gnarled junipers as Ingels' vague shape approached the tent, hailing, 'Jeliff! Get out here! It's the law!'

Deliberately, Luke levered a shell into the rifle's chamber and took aim, laying his sights carefully on the lower line of the black's neck. He squeezed the trigger and was moving aside before the gun's barrel had finished its quick jump. Eight feet out from his first position, he crouched to take aim again, seeing Ingels' black exploding in a sudden lunge. He shot again, his aim this time for the animal's rump.

His bullet must have scorched the gelding, for

the animal reared suddenly, came down on all fours and pitched violently. Ingels, one boot losing a stirrup, lost his seat and fell heavily aground. Luke lined the rifle again and levered three quick shots, his bullets glancing in whining ricochets from the rock a bare foot from Ingels' head.

He didn't wait any longer, but wheeled out of the scrubby cedar and ran for his horse. He dropped the Winchester in a smaller patch of cedar on his quick circle in behind the tent. Then, back there, he drew his .38 and fired once, twice more, before he rode on in at a reckless run toward the tent, calling stridently, 'Ingels!'

'Watch it!' came Ingels' warning shout from behind a tall finger of rock. 'He's off there somewhere!'

'He's gone,' Luke called. 'Had a shot at him as he left. Missed.' He rode up to Ingels. The lawman's gun hung from his hand. He hadn't used it. 'What now?'

'That damned horse of mine! Threw me just as I had my sights laid!' the lawman lied.

'Let me go catch him for you. Better stay away from the tent. I wouldn't swear to it, but I thought I saw a man duck in there when I made my circle. Why'd you come along so soon? I didn't have time to get set.'

'It was over in a minute,' Ingels said mildly, eyeing the tent warily. 'Let's get out of here.'

'Better let me catch up the black first.'

'To hell with that! I'll get on behind you while we look for him.'

The black was wandering aimlessly along the bed of the canyon, reins trailing and broken, his coat glistening wetly below the neck where Luke's first bullet had broken the flesh. Ingels inspected the animal carefully.

'Two damn good shots,' he said at last. 'Maybe we're lucky we didn't stay.'

'Better go back for him, hadn't we?'

'Not on your life! I'm headin' in to tell Geis about this.'

'Maybe I could have a look at the hospital,' Luke said. 'If Parsons can be moved, do I bring him in and lock him up?'

'Yeah. That's a good idea. Need any help?'

Luke shook his head and Ingels rode on. The lawman would have been more than curious to see the smile that came to Luke's face at sight of his headlong run down the canyon. It was plain that Bonanza's sheriff had no stomach for more of what he'd just been through.

The hospital was dark but Luke came down out of the saddle and knocked at the door. It opened instantly and a rifle's barrel snaked out to ram into his stomach. Lifting his hands, he said, 'It's all right, Savage. It's me, Luke.'

Out of the blackness beyond the door, Nan Randall spoke: 'Thank heavens it's you! Let him come in, Fred.'

When the lamp inside was lighted, its glow screened by blankets that had been stretched over the windows, Luke saw that it was Fred Jeliff and not Savage who had answered the door. Back at the alcove, light shone through the slit in the curtains.

Nan held a finger to her lips, telling Luke, 'We must be quiet. The doctor's operating. Parsons may not live. I'll have to get back there and help.' She turned and crossed the room as Jeliff's glance sized up Luke.

Presently, Jeliff said, 'Nan told us about you. What I can't get straight is what good you think it's doin' you to follow Geis around.'

'This much. Ingels and I just paid you a call at your tent. You don't know it, but you were there.' Luke went on to tell the claim-owner of the intended arrest and what had happened at Ingels' approach to the tent. He didn't speak loudly enough for the men on the cots, further along the room, to hear.

Jeliff noticed this and told him, 'Don't worry about Doc's patients. They're all diggin's men. Fact is, Savage is right unpopular these days with the town crowd. We're his only customers.' … He gave Luke a long look that no longer showed the faint suspicion and hostility that had been there at first.… 'You've got my thanks for savin' my outfit. Ingels would sure have burned me out if he'd known the tent was empty.'

'You'll have to hunt up your rifle. It's off there fifty or sixty yards south of the tent. Dropped it in a patch of cedar. Mind tellin' me what went on at Geis's camp tonight?'

Jeliff's long narrow face broke into a wide grin. 'Me and Parsons was the only ones that didn't get off without a scratch. We thought we were pretty smart, leavin' the others and goin' down to cover the trail out of the hideout into the canyon. We must've knocked three or four out of their saddles as they helled out of there, tryin' to dodge the lead Ed and Randall and the others were sendin' down off the rim. That shack must be full enough of holes so that any board'd do for a flour sifter! I saw four men go down. There may be more.'

'How about the gold going out tomorrow?'

'Randall's got everything arranged. I'm riding the stage if this don't give me trouble.' Jeliff lifted his bandaged arm that hung in a sling.

'Then tell Randall I'll be at his place at nine. I ought to be on my way back to town. I'm supposed to be here to arrest Parsons.' ... Luke smiled thinly.... 'But I take it he don't want to be disturbed.'

'I'll tell him to go lock himself up in jail tomorrow, soon as he's walkin' around again,' Jeliff drawled dryly, and the look on his face was a bleak one. It was obvious that he appreciated what Luke was doing, although he didn't say as much openly.

Later, knocking on Geis's office door, Luke heard the saloon-owner's command to enter and opened the door. Geis and Ingels were inside.

'Get him?' Geis asked.

Luke shook his head. 'He was gone. Jeliff, too. I thought about bringin' Savage in but you didn't say anything about him.'

Geis settled back in his chair with a long, almost inaudible sigh. He eyed Luke narrowly for a long moment. Then: 'Better go hit the hay. You want to be in shape to make that drive in the mornin'. Randall's girl going to ride down with you?'

Luke shook his head, detecting a faint sarcasm in the *Nugget* owner's words. But he gave no sign of it. He smiled broadly: 'You won't need me here?'

'Not that I know of. Sam and a few others are watchin' the stage out … just so nothing'll happen on the way.'

Ingels frowned, looking from one to the other, not knowing what lay behind this interchange of words. Luke said good night and went out and for a brief interval after he'd gone Geis sat tilted back in his chair, hands folded across his stomach, deep in thought.

Abruptly, he said, 'Sam, are you sure it wasn't Luke and not Jeliff that threw the lead your way tonight?'

Ingels stiffened on his chair. 'What're you tryin' to say, Matt?'

Geis told him.

87

TWELVE

The buckboard was loaded, or nearly so. George Randall heaved up the last piece, the kitchen table, and helped Luke lash it to the seat-braces. Piled high in the bed of the light rig were blankets, a barrel of china and kitchenware, four chairs and the table, a big and a small chest. The gold was wrapped in the blankets under the seat.

Nancy Randall watched as Luke swung up onto the seat and took the reins her father handed him. George Randall said, 'Good luck, neighbor,' and then Luke was wheeling the team down off the slope of the knoll and into the wagon-road that went down the canyon.

At the bend below he looked back and lifted a hand in a parting salute. The emotion that rose quickly in Nan Randall as she waved back was too strong to be ignored. Here, for the first time, she was consciously aware that this blond-headed stranger with the sure, easy ways had the habit of stirring her deeply, more deeply than any man

88

she had ever known. Realization of her feeling for him was at first frightening, then brought up another that was close to outright happiness.

She asked quietly, 'He'll be all right, won't he, Dad?'

Something in the tone of her voice made George Randall regard her closely. Seeing the high color in her face, the nakedness of emotion in her eyes, he chided, 'You're thinkin' more of him than you are of the gold, Nan!'

Her color deepened and he put his arm about her shoulders and drew her to him. 'He's about as fine as they come,' he said, 'and he'll be back. Now I got to get down to Summers' place and see the stage off. Don't you worry.'

She was glad to be left alone, to search out the new and unexplored vistas that lay open in her mind. Watching her father's retreating back as his spare figure swung down the trail toward the diggin's, she was filled with a wave of thankfulness. Several weeks ago her father had been threatened with physical as well as material ruin. She had saved him from the final break-up and today they were closer than they'd ever been. *If only we could leave Bonanza*, she was thinking, finding it ironical that Luke's departure with most of their possessions was in reality only a pretended leave-taking. The furniture that had left the shack almost bare would be back in place before nightfall. They would stay on here, week after week, until George Randall finally realized the futility of his hope that the near-by hills he'd been prospecting were as poor in gold as his original prospect in the bed of this canyon was rich. Then they'd move on. To where, Nancy didn't care, only so long as they left these squalid diggin's and its memories and such danger as last night's behind them. Her father was man enough to make a new start.

She went inside to clean up the breakfast dishes, thinking of Luke as she set about her work. It was almost an hour later when she heard the thud of hooves on the gravel outside and went to the door to see Doc Savage swinging from the saddle of Fred Jeliff's paint gelding at the hitching-post.

'Howdy, nurse,' he greeted her, his lightness of tone not masking the gravity on his face. 'Feel like joinin' the pony express and takin' a fast ride this mornin'?'

'Something wrong?' she asked him quickly, ignoring his pretended levity.

He nodded. 'Another case of typhoid. Didn't know about it until the stage had left, or I'd have sent this down with the driver.' ... He took an envelope and some money from his pocket.... 'This prescription has to be filled down below at the drug store today. I was thinkin' you could ...'

'I can catch the stage.'

Savage shook his head. 'Better stay away from

the stage. But you could take Jeliff's horse here and go down Rattler and catch your friend in the buckboard.'

'I'll be ready in two minutes.' She turned back into the room. Less than two minutes later she came out the door wearing the waist-overalls and cotton shirt and wide hat that Luke had seen her in his first morning in Bonanza.

The sage-grown trail Luke took to the left three miles below Bonanza angled him through a narrow cleft in the east wall and into a narrow off-shoot that dropped precipitately eastward for better than a mile before it turned south again to follow the general line of the main canyon. He saw immediately why the trail had been abandoned, for the going was rough, crossing ledges of bare rock, skirting countless outcrops in the narrows. Several times he had to stop the team and lead them over bad places. Once he put his shoulder to the wheel to brace it from falling over a twenty-foot-high ledge where the trail climbed the wall.

This was work yet he was somehow glad to be doing it, wanting something to occupy his mind and relieve it of its tangled thinking. That thinking revolved around numerous and unsatisfactory ways of proceeding against Matt Geis once this errand of delivering the gold was accomplished. Reason told him that the wisest thing to do was to ride out, head back for the Brazos and pick up the thread of his old life where he had dropped it before hitting the dark trails ten years ago. That would be a job in itself, for home would be a strange place and old friends would be strangers.

But, stubbornly, he didn't want to leave. Wiping out the stain that was being put on his name seemed now the least of his reasons for not wanting to ride out; in these two days he had laid the groundwork for new friendships that seemed already to make demands on him. There was George Randall, for instance, a man he could regret not having known long before now. There was Doc Savage, whose unselfish attempt to stave off disaster in this unfeeling boom-camp he admired. And there was Nancy Randall.

Thought of this fair-haired girl was stronger than all the others, quickening his interest beyond anything he could remember. He honestly admitted that his feeling for her was stronger than plain liking. At the same time, he bitterly concluded that the obscurity of his back-trail ruled out the possibility of his ever taking a good woman seriously. He could never want his name to cloud that of Nancy Randall; to even think of it galled him. But he could think of her, conjuring up the picture of her clean oval face, the way her hair caught the glint of bright sunlight, her smile that had the habit of bringing up a riot of emotion within him that even now caused a constriction in his throat.

The going smoothed out after the first few miles. But as the team settled to a steady mile-eating trot, the reflected heat of the off-shoot's gaunt rock walls pressed in on him and sent perspiration runneling down the channel of his spine and running down his flat cheeks. He was trained to discomfort, but today's seemed to set up a high-strung nervousness in him. He was restless without knowing why and his habit of scanning what lay ahead and behind was strong now. He laughed aloud once as his squinted straining glance searched the climbing rock tiers of the canyon's west wall, as though some danger lurked there.

He moved a boot from the foot-rail and against the solid bulk of the blanket under the seat, feeling the rounded rawhide sacks wrapped in it, sacks packed with pure rice and flake-gold, a fortune. No one had seen him leave the main trail and no one, not even the deputy at the cottonwood, had been curious about his errand. He knew that Matt Geis was unaccountably suspicious of him; but there was nothing about his errand today to deepen that suspicion, he told himself.

Behind him, shuttling down along Rattler's narrow corridor, came a sound that brought him bolt upright on the seat, tightening on the reins to bring the team to a stand. He caught the sound again, the ring of a running pony's hoofs on rock.

He quickly reined the team over to a low outcrop and jumped aground. He wrapped the reins around a finger of rock, drew the Colt from the holster at his thigh, and put the bulk of another near-by outcropping between him and the stretch of canyon he had covered. Waiting, he wiped his moist palm dry on his shirt time and again, listening to the oncoming rider as the sound of the running animal grew louder. Suddenly the rider swung into view a hundred yards above. And immediately the tension went out of him. For even at this distance he recognized Nancy Randall's erect and graceful shape in the saddle of the paint horse.

He stepped from behind the outcropping, letting his .38 fall back into leather. He lifted a hand and waved.

He was standing that way, arm up-raised, when the sudden air-whip of a bullet brushed his left cheek. Instinctively his long body moved in a lunge, back toward the outcrop, as a rifle's flat explosion echoed down from the rim. His gun streaked from leather as he shouted, 'Back, Nan!'

A hundred feet above on the rim, he caught the glint of sun on metal. His gun arched up, targeting that brightness. He thumbed four swift shots and on the heel of the fourth heard a high-pitched scream and saw a shape straighten from behind a boulder up there, totter on the edge and then come plummeting downward. Fascinated, he watched, momentarily forgetting caution as the rifleman plunged to his death.

He heard Nan's cry and looked her way. Then the solid slam of a bullet took him hard on the back of his left shoulder, its force spinning him around and sending him to his knees. The sound of the shot came a moment later, followed by another as he streaked his gun up once more. Rock and gravel rattled down the near-by talus-slope as the body of the bushwhacker rolled along it. Up-canyon, he saw a figure move out from the wall toward Nancy. A shot sounded from up there and he had a swift glimpse of the paint horse going to its knees in a thrashing fall, throwing the girl clear.

Then, as he faced the rim and looked above once more, a voice called from behind him: 'Drop that iron, Barron! *Pronto*, or I bust your spine!'

Wariness, a long training in not trying to outface too-strong odds, loosened his grip on the gun. He brought his hands up, turning as he moved them and grimacing against the pain in his left shoulder.

Facing him from across the canyon stood Sam Ingels, a sawed-off shotgun at his shoulder. There was a smile of triumph on the lawman's face as he stepped across toward Luke. He glanced up-canyon, called, 'Bring her along, Mart!'

THIRTEEN

Ed Tyler was bored and restless this morning, having watched from the rim above Randall's shack Luke's preparations and departure and George Randall's leave-taking of his daughter a few minutes later. Ed, whose make-up demanded a certain amount of action to stalemate boredom, felt at a loose end this morning. He had slept under the stars last night, slept soundly up here back of the rim above Randall's shack. His horse was staked out in a shallow coulee a dozen rods beyond where he now lay in the shade of a cedar, watching the shack below.

He made and smoked out half a dozen cigarettes in the long interval after Nancy had disappeared inside the shack, wondering idly how much damage the state-guards could do Geis's men before they gave up the almost certain fight that would take place down the canyon.

His attention was brought sharply back to the shack at Doc Savage's appearance and Nan's hasty departure on the paint horse. Curious, a little worried at this unexpected development, Ed decided to follow the girl. He saddled quickly and took a faintly marked trail along the rim that looked down on first the diggin's and then the town. He overtook the girl as she was entering the upper limits of the street. Although he couldn't follow her along it, he worked on the theory that she might be going down-canyon and rode further until he came abreast the cottonwood under which the deputy's gunstand stood. Presently, Nancy Randall came along the trail, passed the cottonwood and ran her paint horse down-canyon.

Ed tried to hail her, but the drumming pound of her pony's hooves must have kept her from hearing. He was working his way down off the rim, two miles below town, when he saw her take the trail into the off-shoot that led down Rattler. He was ten minutes behind her in taking that branching and only well within ear-shot when the echo of the guns rattled up the canyon's high corridor.

The sound of those guns at first made him gouge his mare cruelly with spurs, then pull the animal to an abrupt halt. At times like this, he always tried to pattern his behaviour in the way he thought Luke Barron would have patterned his, and now he knew that to rush headlong at those guns below was more foolish than brave.

So he tied the mare back out of sight in a deep

indentation in the wall and went on afoot, warily, hurrying across the open spaces that didn't have any cover. He walked almost a quarter of a mile until, shielded by the vertical buttress of a sharp turning, he came in sight of Luke and Nan and the three men who faced them.

One of these Ed recognized immediately as the sheriff. The others were deputies, he supposed. The distance to where they stood, to where a fourth was approaching, leading their horses, was a good hundred yards. It was too great a distance for accurate shooting with a six-gun and Ed cursed impotently at not having brought along a rifle ... until he happened to remember that he hadn't owned one for a year.

The best he could do was to watch. Presently, the sheriff and one of his men went across to the buckboard and began throwing its contents out onto the ground, while the two remaining men held their guns lined at Luke and Nan, who were standing together. Ed saw Luke clenching his left shoulder and knew that his friend had stopped a bullet. He tried helplessly to think of a way of working closer to those four men, within range of them, but in the end gave it up. There was no cover between him and them.

He heard the sheriff shout and saw him stand upright in the buckboard, lifting the heavy weight of the blanket-wrapped gold to the seat. After that, things happened swiftly. The gold was divided and stuffed into saddle-pouches on the sheriff's and a deputy's horse, after which Nan and Luke were put astride the backs of the buckboard team, which was cut out of harness. Ingels took pains in roping his prisoners' feet under the bellies of their horses.

Then, as Ed was crouching behind the rock buttress, his gun already cocked in expectation of taking the sheriff and his men by surprise when they rode back up the canyon, he saw the six riders turn down canyon and go out of sight around a further bend.

He ran back to his pony and followed warily, passing the spot where the dead paint pony lay and the empty buckboard stood with its load littering the ground nearby. For two miles beyond he followed the tracks in the thin sandy top-soil, going warily, having to ride slowly. Finally he came to a ledge-trail where the sign he was following climbed to the canyon's west rim. Topping that, he scanned a mile-wide mesa in time to see Luke and Nan and their guards disappear over the far edge and down a side-trail that entered the main canyon.

By two that afternoon, he was certain enough of their destination to break off his pursuit and head back for town. Ingels and his men were taking Luke and the girl to the hideout Ed and the claim-owners had raided last night. They had ridden north out of the canyon and passed Bonanza and the diggin's.

He found George Randall at the shack and briefly gave him the story. Within another half hour, Randall had gathered eight men in the yard out front and was posting them on what had happened. Three of these men had ridden guard on the stage this morning and had returned with it to town after driving the whole length of the canyon without being stopped. All eight had sent gold down in the buckboard. All eight listened to Randall and Ed with a blending of helpless rage and alarm on their faces.

As Randall ended his story, one of them spoke up sharply, 'George, you've been fooled the same as the rest. We ain't blamin' you for what happened. But I think I've got this straight now. This here gent we been callin' Luke is really Luke Barron! Ain't he, Tyler?'

Ed nodded, impulsively deciding that it was best for them to know the whole truth.

But before he had a chance to make his explanations, the speaker went on: 'And, by God, you got the gall to stand there and admit it!' In sudden inexplicable rage, the man struck out at Ed. Ed wasn't looking for the blow. It caught him on the point of the chin, rocked his head back. His knees buckled and he fell to the ground, unconscious.

'What the hell, Bill?' George Randall cried.

Bill said, 'Keep your nose out o' this, Randall! It wasn't your gold that was lost. It was ours!' ... He swung around on the others ... 'The rest of you get this and get it quick! This here Ed Tyler admits he traveled with Barron across in Colorado. You heard him admit this jasper we trusted with our gold was the real Luke Barron. Can't you see what we done?'

'Goddlemighty!' Frank Summers muttered, as Bill Olds' idea came home to him. 'You mean Barron stole our gold?'

'Not only that, he had the gall to send Tyler down here, and try to toll us off the scent and keep us busy while he made his getaway! It's been Barron all along! I hate Matt Geis's guts about as bad as any man here. But except for his chargin' us money for rotten whiskey and good water, we don't have a thing against Geis!'

'Easy, Bill,' Doc Savage said. 'It looks to me like Tyler was telling the truth. This Luke, even if he is Luke Barron, was tryin' to help us.'

It was Frank Summers' mirthless laugh that mocked the medico's words and convinced the others. 'You get Tyler patched up while we take care of this other, Doc,' he drawled, seeing the medico kneeling alongside Ed, who still lay unconscious under Bill Olds' blow. 'Randall, you better not come along.'

'Along where?' Bill Olds queried.

'First, to that camp we raided last night. Ten to one says we don't find Ingels or anyone else in it. If we don't, if Tyler was runnin' the sandy I think

101

he was, we'll go down Rattler and pick up what sign we can and follow it out before dark. That is, if any of you expect to get your pokes back again.'

Randall and Savage argued but the others wouldn't listen. These men had all their worldly possessions at stake now. Even if Ed hadn't been knocked out, they wouldn't have listened to his explanation about Luke. They were men half crazed by the loss of their gold, men who thought they'd been made fools of at the hands of an outlaw, and at this moment there wasn't one who didn't firmly believe that Luke Barron was responsible for all that had happened these past weeks.

As Frank Summers put it, arguing with Randall: 'George, I'm sorry about your girl. We'll do the best we can to get her back. But you know what's happened. This Luke Barron's been here all the time, workin' on the quiet, puttin' the blame on Geis and Ingels. He waited for a chance to make a really big haul. He showed himself for the first time, made a big play against Geis and the law to get in with us. We trusted him. Hell, we even hand our gold to him and say, "Here, Luke, go on all by yourself and take this with you!" Why, damn it, there ain't a man here that has half a brain.'

'You're wrong, Frank, dead wrong,' Randall stated miserably.

That was the end of the talk. Frank Summers

led his men down the trail from the shack. They were on their way to get guns and horses. Randall knew that if they did meet Luke today, the outlaw wouldn't stand a chance against them.

Randall was feeling miserable, helpless. He went over to Savage, who was working over Ed. Savage looked up at him and smiled sympathetically. 'I know how you feel, George. We all made a mistake. But Nan will be all right.'

'You mean you believe that trash about Luke Barron!'

Savage nodded soberly. 'It's plain as the nose on your face, George. We've been taken for a bunch of suckers.'

'But, damn it! ...' Randall broke off, helpless before the futility of trying again to explain. He was himself certain that Luke hadn't betrayed them. But he was powerless to convince others. He said calmly, 'Can you bring him around?' nodding down to Ed.

'If I had some whiskey it might help.'

Randall went into the shack and returned with a full pint of whiskey. He helped pour some down Ed's throat. As Ed opened his eyes, Randall corked the bottle and shoved it in his hip pocket. Savage noted with surprise that Randall hadn't touched the liquor himself. And if a man ever needed a drink now, Randall, a drinking man until two weeks ago, did.

FOURTEEN

A long four-hour ride after climbing the narrow trail out of Rattler, Sam Ingels called a halt near the only patch of green vegetation they had seen in many miles that lay behind. At the western edge of a shallow basin, close in to the foot of a pock-marked sandy cliff, was a spring that bubbled to the surface of the ground, ran a few feet through a willow-thicket and then sank out of sight again, leaving only a fanning-out patch of moist sand to mark its course.

Luke was unable to stand for a moment after they lifted him from the saddle. His legs were numb below the knees. His shoulder ached like a tooth with the nerve exposed. His sleeve the length of his arm was crimson with blood. Nan, whose face had been etched in pain the last few miles from the tightness of the rope that bound her boots together under the belly of her horse, forgot her own misery and came quickly across to him, saying, 'Lie down, Luke. Let me fix your shoulder.'

Sam Ingels drawled, 'That's right, sister! Fix him up. We'll need him later on.'

The lawman had remained taciturn and aloof during the ride in through this gaunt maze of badlands far west of the main canyon's flanking mesa. He had ignored Luke's protest over being roped to her animal and when the girl once wanted to stop to bandage Luke's bad arm he gave no sign that he had heard, only urging them on faster. It was plain that he wanted to reach their goal quickly.

Instead of taking his two prisoners to the hideout in the canyon above the diggin's, he had followed what Luke supposed was the trail to the hideout almost to its end before swinging sharply west over a wide shelf of bare rock that would hide their signs. They had travelled that direction across the wide mesa that formed the canyon's west shoulder, finally dipping down from it into this rocky weather-eroded maze of badlands. Luke judged they had ridden through this series of broken buttes and narrow canyons for almost ten miles, keeping to a westerly direction. Wind and rain and sun had eroded this land so that the soft sandy rock had taken on fantastic shapes and color. The beds of the washes were strewn with tall monuments where harder strata of rock had withstood the centuries-long battle against the elements. The cliff faces showed many indentations, caves of all proportions, while the reds

105

and browns and yellows of the bare rock made vivid splashes of color.

Just now, as Nan went to the spring for water, Ingels came to stand straddle-legged looking down at Luke, who sat hunched over, his good hand clenching his throbbing arm tightly. 'Good thing that slug was four inches out,' the lawman drawled. 'I didn't think of it at the time, but maybe we can use you after all.'

When Luke made no reply, Ingels glanced across at his men and gave them a knowing wink, continuing: 'Matt'll think up something. Maybe a hangin'. Or maybe turnin' you over to the mob. That was you that shot up my horse last night, wasn't it?'

He put his question suddenly. Luke pretended ignorance, looking up and asking, 'You mean Jeliff?'

The sheriff eyed him coldly a moment, knowing the information he wanted wasn't to be forthcoming. He heard the girl coming up behind him, turned and eyed her with a smug smile. He jerked a thumb toward the precipitous face of the cliff. 'Which room'll you have, Miss? Sorry we ain't got any with bath.'

Nan looked toward the cliff face, where a series of narrow ledges led upward toward a maze of cave-like openings. Luke understood immediately what the sheriff meant. Those holes were the openings to cave-dwellings, occupied centuries

ago by Indians who had probably cultivated this
small basin when the flow of the spring was much
stronger, giving them water for their meagre
crops.

The girl ignored Ingels and knelt beside Luke,
washing clean the hole in his shoulder just over
the line of the collar-bone. She made a compress of
her handkerchief and bound it tightly to the
wound with Luke's neck-piece. Although she
didn't speak, there was a tenderness in her touch
and a warmth in her glance he knew she intended
to be encouraging.

'No bones busted, eh, sister?' Ingels queried,
having watched her.

'No.'

Ingels nodded to one of his men. 'Then tie him
up, Mart.'

One of the deputies came forward. Nan said
sharply, 'You can't do that! He's hurt! Badly! It
might ... might kill him!'

'Now wouldn't that be too bad!' the lawman
drawled, and Luke saw in him a man different
than the Matt Geis understrapper he knew.
Without Geis's authority to override him, Sam
Ingels was showing a talent at cold-bloodedness.
The smile he now gave the girl broadened, and he
added: 'Better lace her up again, too, Mart.'

Luke made one weak attempt to get to his feet,
thinking that if he could stand he might somehow
manage to get his hands on the gun of the man

who was to tie him. But he was pushed roughly back again, another came across to help Mart Kemp, and presently both his arms were bound tightly to his sides and many windings of stout manila held his boots and legs together. He had to lie there and watch Nan undergo the indignity of receiving the same treatment.

They were carried up a narrow ledge to the lowest row of cave-openings. Luke lay on the hot rock watching them drag Nan out of sight through one opening. Then he was roughly carried and pushed in through the adjoining one.

He found himself lying in a dome-shaped room. The roof of the cave was black from the smoke of long-extinct fires. A small opening high on the front wall to one side of the door was the chimney that had centuries ago let the smoke of the fires escape. In the back wall was gouged a deep niche that must have served as a shelf for food. Around the wall ran a regular zig-zag pattern cut in the rock, a symbol or decoration for this crude home.

Ingels, kneeling and looking in through the opening, gave Luke a parting word of warning. He spoke to his deputy: 'Mart, you're stayin' on with 'em. He may try to break out. Build your fire so's it'll light up this ledge. Have your rifle handy. If he shows his head outside, part his hair in a new place with a bullet.' His glance swung down on Luke, who lay against the back wall. '*Sabe, amigo?*'

'What about the girl?' Luke asked.

Ingels shrugged, his moustached face taking on a wry smile. 'Matt decides that,' he said. 'Maybe he can make a deal with Randall. He's noticed her before.'

He laughed softly as he saw the look of sudden rage on Luke's face and told his deputy, 'Let's go.'

Luke lay breathing heavily, filled with a sense of utter helplessness, for in the ten years of precarious living since Texas had outlawed him he had never been in a spot like this, one in which he hadn't been able to think out even a likely chance for fighting his way out. There wasn't a chance now, he knew. Matt Geis would use him as proof of the genuineness of the Luke Barron scare that had struck terror through Bonanza. But he wasn't thinking of that. The fear for Nan Randall's safety crowded everything else from his mind.

Lying there, almost blinded by his helpless rage, he was brought back to sudden sanity by the sound of the girl's voice close at hand. It seemed to be coming from the far wall of the cave, in the direction of the opening he had seen her carried into. He lifted his head and looked across there. What he saw brought him rigid in the grip of a faint but nevertheless real hope.

At the base of the sand-drifted wall across there was a narrow slitted opening through which a sliver of light shone. He could hear her voice plainly now, saying, '... leave him there to die! He needs water, something to eat!'

And Sam Ingels' reply sounded through the opening just as plainly. 'He'll get water, sister. And he'll get food. Didn't I say we need him later on?'

'But his arm! It's tied. There's danger of infection.'

'Ever see a man die of blood poisonin'?' Ingels asked. 'I have. It takes four or five days. That's long enough for us to be finished with him.'

Luke heard the girl's choked cry, then the strike of boots as Ingels and his deputy went back down the ledge.

All at once he had forgotten the pain of his shoulder. He lifted his knees and pushed himself through the sand toward the opening onto the ledge. As he worked his way across there, he was remembering the pattern of other cave-dwellings he'd seen years ago when he was a boy. They were invariably of the same pattern, one or two room caves gouged into the face of soft-rock cliffs. The rooms, if more than one, were connected by low arched passageways. The slit through which the light had shone in from Nan's cave had been the top of such a passageway showing above the sand that had drifted in to fill the caves to ledge-height in the long centuries since their use.

It cost him a long effort and a torment of pain to push his way to the opening so that he could lie belly-down and lift his head and peer over the ledge and downward. Down there, Ingels and two of his men were climbing into their saddles, getting ready to leave. Three horses were tied in the willows, that of the deputy who was staying behind and the buckboard team. Ingels spoke to the man who was to remain, Kemp, but Luke couldn't distinguish his words. Once Ingels pointed above toward the narrow ledge and the cave and Kemp's answer was a significant slapping of his palm on the stock of the .30-.30 Winchester he held cradled in the crook of his arm. Shortly, Ingels and the other pair rode away, Ingels' and the other man's saddle-pouches bulging with the bulk of the gold that had been taken out of the blanket from under the seat of George Randall's buckboard.

FIFTEEN

Long afterward the sheriff and his deputies rode
out of sight into the mouth of a narrow wash far
across the basin. Below, Kemp was preparing his
camp, gathering dead cedar from a grove of
stunted trees a few yards above the spring at the
foot of the cliff. Then he disappeared up a
climbing ledge that took the direction opposite
this one. He was back presently, carrying
blankets, a lantern, a frying pan, a sack of flour
and a blanket-slung burden that proved a
moment later to contain all the possibles for
preparing a simple meal. There were tin plates
and cups, even knives and forks. There were
rusted tin cans that must have held salt and
baking-powder. And there were several handfuls
of jerky. Luke guessed correctly that this camp
had been used before this by Ingels' men, that the
food had been cached on some previous visit to
these caves.

The hope that had been in him at sight of the

inside opening to Nan's cave grew stronger. Yet he wasn't willing to act on it yet. He could have called through the opening to Nan but didn't, afraid that she might betray his discovery to the deputy by some look or sign when he brought their evening meal, which he now set about preparing. Luke crawled to the back of the cave again, more aware of the pain in his shoulder now. He dropped off into a restless doze.

Kemp's entrance into the cave woke him. The deputy carried the lantern in one hand, a plate of food holding jerky, pan-break and a steaming cup of coffee in the other. It was dark outside and the glare of the lantern blinded Luke for a moment.

The deputy's glance took in the marks in the sand. When he drawled, 'Been movin' around, eh?' Luke was immediately thankful that he hadn't crawled over to the opening to Nan's cave, for the tell-tale marks in the sand would have aroused the deputy's suspicions.

'Here. I'll let your arms loose.' Kemp lifted Luke to a sitting position after setting down the plate of food. He pointedly drew the heavy .45 from his holster, moving around behind Luke and began working at the knots in the rope. As it came free and Luke could move his arms Kemp moved quickly out of reach and squatted on his heels near the door, adding the information: 'Your partner's already fed. She's sure worried about you, Barron. Tough you ain't goin' to be able to promote that.'

Luke's immediate reaction was one of anger. But he put that down before a thought that made him smile thinly and drawl, 'I may yet.'

Curious, the deputy said, 'Like to make a bet on it?' He lifted his Colt in a gesture packed with meaning.

Luke had a part to play here, chiefly to put up the appearance that he was trying to find a way of escape by any means. So he went on with his first thought, saying abruptly, 'You and me could take over that town, Kemp!'

The deputy smiled broadly. It was plain that he was enjoying this leading on of his prisoner as he queried blandly, 'How?'

'We know Ingels and Geis have the gold. They'll meet sometime tonight to split it with their crew.'

'Correct. The meetin's called for midnight at the *Nugget!*' ... Kemp gave the information willingly, relishing the rashness of sharing this confidence with a man who couldn't use it ... 'So what?'

'The two of us could bust in through the back window to Geis's office, throw down on that pack and take the gold right out from under their noses.'

'Y'don't say!' Masking his real thoughts, the deputy pretended surprise. 'Just you and me, eh?'

'I could get one more man to help us. Tyler, the one that broke jail a couple days ago.'

The deputy's stare widened in mock bewilderment. 'Now don't tell me you busted him out!'

Luke nodded gravely, wolfing down his food.

'I thought Ingels was stringin' me along. You mean you're really this Luke Barron?'

The awe Kemp tried to put into his expression looked far from genuine. Luke ignored that, soberly continuing this double-edged pretense. 'The same.'

'Then it's been you all along? Not someone else usin' your handle?'

Luke shook his head at the question. 'No. Someone's been usin' my handle all right. I came in here to put a stop to it. But here's my idea now. Get rid of Geis and Ingels, get our hands on the gold. Then we keep on with this Luke Barron idea, take the whole diggin's over and ...'

Suddenly a loud guffaw of the deputy's cut in on his words. He looked at the man with mock anger on his face. He tried to say something but the deputy's laugh drowned out his voice. Then, when Kemp paused laughing long enough to get his breath, he asked flatly, 'What the hell is this? You think I'm runnin' a sandy?'

'Hell, no! You're dead serious, you poor blind sucker! Think I'd take a flyer like this when I'm already in on a sure thing with Geis?' ... Laughter came again, more scornfully now.... 'Go ahead with your eatin'. I'll bust a gut if you don't!'

It was hard for Luke to keep on with the pretense, to make his face take on the unaccustomed sullen look he knew should be his reaction to the deputy's derision. But he did a fair job of it. For as Kemp moved in behind to tie the rope again, the plate empty now, he drawled: 'You must've been up against some pretty weak-minded jaspers across there in Colorado. You ain't even dry behind the ears yet, Barron! Me sling in with you!'

He was smiling derisively again as he picked up the plate and lantern and crawled out of the low opening. He paused outside on the ledge and called back, 'Scared of the dark, Barron?'

When Luke made no reply, the deputy's mocking laugh came again. Minutes later Luke hunched over to the ledge-opening to look down and see him lying back with his head on his saddle close to the fire smoking a cigarette.

There was no need to wait any longer. Favoring his hurt shoulder, Luke pushed across to the slitted opening to Nan's cave. He put his mouth close to it and called, 'Nan!'

'I'm here,' came her whispered answer, close beyond. 'I wondered if you knew about this. What are we going to do?'

'I'm coming through,' Luke told her. 'Move back a little.'

'I'll dig from my side,' was her answer and he heard her stir in the darkness beyond the opening.

He began the laborious effort of moving his boots around to the opening. When he could feel it with the toe of one boot, he started digging at the sand with his heels, scooping it back from the opening by bending his knees. The fine sand was dry, loosely-packed, and came away easily. The hardest part came with having to move the scooped-out sand to one side so that it wouldn't sift back into the widening opening. He did that by working around at right angles and pushing the piled sand to one side with his feet.

In the long interval he lay there working against the tautness of the ropes that bound his legs together, his shoulder stabbed time and again with a knife-like pain that crowded in over the continuous throbbing hurt. A beady perspiration stood out on his forehead and ran into his eyes. It was a long sheer torment that he fought with all the force of his will. Many times it seemed easier to lie back and close his eyes, letting the pain in his shoulder ease off. But each time he did that he would remember the threat represented by the deputy lying by the fire below; and each time he hesitated he could hear Nan Randall working at the opening from her side. So he struggled on, not minding the way the rope cut into his legs and numbed his feet.

Finally he reached out with his boots and thrust them through the opening. They had cleared away almost a foot of the sand now. He felt Nan's boot prod his a moment later and called softly, 'Can you work your back in to my feet and get at the knot? Can you move your hands?'

She was a brief moment in replying, hesitantly, 'I ... I don't know. I can't feel them any more.'

'Try,' he told her and lay there trying to follow her movements as the pressure of her body moved against his boots.

It seemed an eternity before he felt her fingers move the knotted rope around his boots. He said, 'Good girl!' hoping this small encouragement would help.

Once, in the long minutes that followed, she paused and he heard her breathing deeply from the effort it was costing her to work at the stubborn knot. 'No hurry, Nan. Rest a minute,' he called.

'Is your shoulder hurting?' she asked, her tone full of concern.

'Not much.'

'I think I'll have it this time.' Her hands were working at the knot again.

Suddenly Luke felt the tightness of the rope slack away from his boots. He pulled them back through the opening and moved his legs and the rope fell away. 'Now the other,' he told her, edging quickly into the opening and arching his back to force his upper body against it.

He felt her hands touch one of his and clench it with a pressure that told him that the same wild hope was in her that had come to him. Then, almost before he realized it, the first winding of the rope about his arms came loose and he was

pushing up to a sitting position and elbowing out
the windings of the stout half-inch manila.

He moved his good arm gingerly at first,
starting the circulation in it. Then he rubbed the
other, relishing the relief of the throbbing easing
out of his shoulder.

'Comin' through,' he called, and crawled into
the opening.

He had to try twice before he could force his
shoulders through, wincing at the pain of his bad
shoulder wedged in the opening. Then he was
crawling through the hole and in beside Nan, his
hands working swiftly to untie her.

SIXTEEN

From the low opening of Nan's cave, they looked down on the fire below the ledge. It had burned low, to a bed of live red coals. Kemp sat a few feet out from it toward the willow-thicket, arms folded on knees, head lowered. Nearby was the pile of brush he had gathered to feed the fire. Off in the darkness to the right was where Luke had seen the horses tied earlier but the shadows down there were too dense for him to make them out now.

Nan said in a whisper: 'He's asleep.' She was gingerly rubbing her left wrist where a winding of the rope had burned the skin.

'Dozing,' Luke told her. 'He'll be up in a minute to fix the fire. We'll have to move fast.' As he spoke he reached out of the opening and picked up a fist-sized rock that lay on the ledge.

The glance Nan gave him was full of mixed fear and hope. In the faint starlight the expression on her oval face was one of complete trust and as his eyes met hers she leaned closer to him so that her shoulder pressed against his. The girl was afraid but trying not to show it; she needed the acute awareness of his presence beside her to assure her that the danger threatening wasn't as ominous as it looked. There seemed to be no way for them to get out of the caves, with the likelihood of the deputy waking at any moment.

She asked softly, 'Could I call him up here?'

He shook his head. 'Might tip him off that something was wrong.'

He reached out and opened her hand and put the rock in it ... 'I'm going down. Give me a two minute start, then toss this down the ledge. If it doesn't wake him, toss another. He's got to be looking up here while I move in on him.'

She breathed quickly, 'Luke! You have to be careful! You can't ...' She caught herself, abruptly stifling the panic in her voice. Then she smiled up at him as she added, more quietly, 'I'll do it. Good luck.'

Luke pulled off his boots, said, 'Keep your fingers crossed!' and crawled out the opening, coming erect on the ledge. He flattened to the sheer climbing wall and moved soundlessly along the narrow shelf to the right of the fire. These few seconds were the ones that counted, for even the faint light of the coals was enough to outline him plainly against the sand-colored wall. If Kemp's doze was genuine, he was safe enough. But if the deputy was only pretending to be asleep, having heard them moving around and suspecting something gone wrong, then Luke was in as tight a spot as Ingels and Geis intended he should be a day or two from now, faced by a Bonanza mob that would hang him.

His nerves were tight-drawn with wariness. He put all the keen alertness of his hunted years into the immediate task of moving as quietly as a shadow. His darting glance moved from the fire to the ledge and back again as he carefully chose each spot to place a foot before going on. And with all his caution, he moved fast. He was ten feet out from the cave, fifteen, twenty, and here the fire's meagre light failed to lift the shadows. The ledge dropped steeply. He was beyond the open space edging this side of the fire and above the willow-thicket. Twenty more feet and he would be off the ledge and behind the impenetrable screen of willows, hidden from sight of the fire.

Kemp's head all at once jerked up. The deputy's glance at once lifted to the ledge, inspecting it carefully. Then he pushed his Stetson onto the back of his head, scrubbed his eyes with an open palm and stretched, yawning. His unsuspecting glance swung around and seemed to focus directly on Luke, who had flattened rigid to the wall.

Then, lazily, Kemp came to his feet and sauntered over to lift an arm-load of brush from the pile and toss it onto the fire. The rustle and cracking of the dry wood drowned out the slurring sifting of pebbles Luke's foot kicked loose as he covered those last few feet in swift strides down off the ledge.

The soft damp earth in the willows hid his move as he approached the fire from behind. He was at Kemp's back now, looking out from the edge of the willows as the deputy stood in the light of the catching blaze and rolled a smoke. Back there a few steps Luke had moved too violently and hurt his wounded shoulder. Now he thrust his left hand into his shirt and let it hang there as in a sling to ease the renewed throb that sent lances of pain along the thick shoulder muscle into his neck.

He heard the sudden loud rattle of the rock along the ledge. As the sound wiped out the acute silence, Kemp's two hands came alive, dropping the half-rolled cigarette, right stabbing to his thigh. Two swift lunging strides carried the deputy back out of the firelight to the edge of the willows, where he crouched, palming out his .45.

Four feet behind him, Luke momentarily heard his quick breathing and the low-voiced oath that escaped him. Then Luke moved out, right fist swinging an arc that began its travel at knee-height. Kemp heard that move behind him and began a rising turn that took him up out of his crouch, his Colt lifting. Luke's fist caught him full on the point of the jaw, lifting him up and backward. The Colt exploded groundward, its bullet geysering sand a bare four inches from Luke's left boot.

Kemp's knees buckled and he fell face down, rolling onto his back. His eyes were open in the glazed stare of unconsciousness as Luke pried the gun from his clenched hand.

Luke called, 'Come on down, Nan! Bring the rope,' as he knelt alongside the deputy and made sure that he was still alive.

He looked toward the caves and saw Nan's slender shape moving along the ledge. A moment later she was running across toward him, the firelight edging her head with flaming gold. She stood in front of him, staring unbelievingly as she said in a hushed voice: 'I thought ... I was afraid he'd ...'

All at once the emotion in her was too strong to be stemmed. Her words choked off as the tension went out of her. And, before Luke knew it had happened, her arms were around him tightly and her head was against his shoulder and he could feel the fight she made to stifle the sobbing that came against her will.

He tilted her head up. 'We're out of it.'

Presently she drew away from him, blinking the tears back. She smiled. 'I'm silly. I knew all along you'd do it. What happens now?'

'Make Kemp comfortable first. Then we go back to town after the gold.' He glanced upward at the stars. It was a little past ten. 'The gold?' she asked. 'I thought the sheriff took it with him.'

'He did. But Kemp let me in on a little something that may help us get it back.'

'Not a sign of 'em,' Ed Tyler said ruefully, emerging from the shack at Geis's hideout up the canyon. 'George, this looks bad!'

His statement only deepened George Randall's gloom. The two of them had come up here on the hopeless chance that Frank Summers and the other claim-owners had overlooked something in their quick visit this afternoon. They had approached the hideout warily, late, thinking that Ingels might wait until then to bring his prisoners down. But they found the camp deserted, the bullet-holes peppered on the sides of the shack during last night's raid the only visible evidence that it had been recently occupied.

Behind Ed through the doorway, Randall caught the flickering glow of flames. He nodded, said briefly, 'I didn't think of that,' knowing that Ed had started a blaze inside that would soon burn the shack to the ground.

They stepped wearily into the saddle and started back down the canyon toward the diggin's, the glow of the burning shack glowing redly in darkness behind. It was late, nearly midnight. Somewhere far below Frank Summers and the claim-owners would be around a fire restlessly waiting out the night so that at dawn they could follow out the sign leading from the abandoned buckboard in Rattler.

A jumble of thoughts tortured George Randall. Strongest was a stark fear that he might never see his daughter again. Weakest was a devilish distrust of Ed Tyler and Luke Barron. He didn't want to believe that Ed and Luke had betrayed their friends; but Frank Summers and his men had strong arguments to back this supposition. After all, wasn't he trusting Ed Tyler's word against that of the others? What real proof was there against Matt Geis and Sam Ingels except the raid on the hideout last night and Geis's stubborn refusal to let go his hold on his well? Hadn't Luke built up all this proof against their suspicions of Geis? Couldn't it be that Geis, blamed unfairly for what was going on here, was waging a natural fight against men he was powerless to prevent becoming his enemies?

Randall swore viciously, damning the workings of his mind.

'What's eatin' you, George?' Ed queried, reining in to let the prospector come up with him.

Before he quite knew what he was doing, Randall was blurting out the truth, working the torment of his mind.

Ed listened with a look of rimrock hardness freezing his square features. 'Sure, I know how you feel,' he drawled as Randall finished. He shrugged. 'All I can say is to wait and see. If Luke can move a muscle, we still have a chance.'

'But if he's dead! Then what?'

'Then you and me don't stand any more chance than crickets in a grass-fire!'

Ed's bleak admission did more to stem the distrust in Randall's mind than anything that had so far happened. He asked himself what, if Luke Barron was in back of all this, was the point in Ed Tyler remaining behind and going through this pretense. If Luke had stolen the gold this afternoon, there was nothing to be gained in sending his lieutenant back to try and cover his deed before the men he had robbed. All at once Randall's last doubt was wiped out. He had his answer. Luke Barron and Ed Tyler weren't in back of this.

Up ahead, Ed called back abruptly, 'Did we leave a light on, George?'

Randall came even with him and into sight of the shack down the canyon. The back window was lighted, its shade drawn. 'No. Who could it be?' he spoke absently, asking himself the question rather than Ed.

'You take the front, I'll work in from the back. Better go right on in and forget your gun,' was Ed's advice.

Randall followed the suggestion, leaving Ed and riding straight down the canyon, making no attempt to hide his approach as he climbed the knoll. Coming up across the yard, he called, 'Hello! Anyone there?'

The door swung abruptly open on Nan. 'Dad!' she cried, and ran out to him. As he took her in his arms, Ed came around the far corner of the shack, dropping his gun back into holster. Standing near the window at the rear of the shack, he had heard Randall's hail and the girl's answer.

Inside, Luke came up off a chair as they entered. He had taken off his blood-stained shirt, which lay on a chair by the stove. His shoulder was swathed in clean bandages.

Ed grinned broadly at sight of him, saying, 'What'd I tell you, George? He's a hard man to kill. Goin' to tell us about it, Luke?'

Luke didn't but Nan did, telling of their escape, of leaving Kemp thoroughly roped and lying in the willow-thicket so as to save him from tomorrow's hot sun, and of their ride back out of the badlands and across the mesa. 'And Luke says we have a chance to get the gold back,' the girl ended by saying.

At Randall's quizzical glance, Luke nodded. 'Kemp didn't know I could ever use the information. Geis's men are meeting with him at midnight, at the *Nugget*, to make the split.'

Randall took out his watch and looked at it. 'Quarter of an hour,' he said. 'I'll get you a shirt and we can be on our way.' The change in Randall during the past few minutes was pronounced. He seemed a younger man now that hope was in him and the worry over Nan's safety was lifted from his mind. Of them all, he was the most eager to be on the way to the *Nugget*.

As Luke was gingerly pulling the sleeve of one of Randall's too-small shirts onto his bad arm, he paused suddenly as the sound of distant gunshots echoed up along the canyon.

The rest heard it. Randall stepped over and opened the door and listened. There were several more shots, distance-muted but clear.

'Comin' from town,' the prospector said. 'Nothin' to ...'

A prolonged rattle of guns cut in on his words. Luke made a sudden motion of pulling on the shirt and buttoning it. With swift, sure moves he palmed the .45 from the holster he'd taken from Kemp, rocked open the loading-gate and spun the cylinder, inspecting the loads.

Then his slow drawl brought them all up tense: 'Better get down there, hadn't we?'

SEVENTEEN

Late afternoon saw Frank Summers and ten other claim-owners approaching the abandoned buckboard four miles down Rattler canyon. The dead paint horse lay well out from the bend. Near it, Summers, in the lead, lifted a hand in a signal that halted the others. They ringed him and his glance went around the circle of faces. 'Bill, you and Nels go on ahead,' he said. 'And go careful. You know sign better'n any of us. See how it tallies with what Tyler told us. There's Fred's paint, which is like Tyler said we'd find it. Begin with that.'

Bill Olds nodded to Nels Larsen, an old Swede well acquainted with these hills, and swung down out of his saddle, handing his reins to the nearest man. As Larsen headed down toward the buckboard, Olds approached the paint, made a wide circle around the carcass and then went closer to study the hole made by the bullet that had killed the animal. Squatting there on his heels, the others saw his glance lift to the rim, then lower again to observe something more carefully.

Finally he called across, 'Rifle brought him down. Here's the tracks of the man that shot him.' … He lifted a hand and waved toward the narrow canyon's east wall. … 'He shot from over there. The girl took a bad spill and this jasper came out and got her. She must've put up a scrap. Sand's kicked around plenty. What'd you find, Nels?' he called.

Larsen walked back from the buckboard toward them. There was a puzzled frown on his face. Walking up, he told them, 'Danged if it ain't like he said it'd be. Two men came across to take another that'd forted up behind some rock over the wall. The print where he dropped his gun is plain. Must've been Barron. Harness is cut on the rig. They took off down the canyon after gatherin' a couple more that come down from above. The girl was one of 'em, or else it was a man with powerful small feet.'

Summers' glance went to his men. He saw the puzzlement on their faces and admitted finally, 'Looks like I was wrong. Tyler was tellin' the truth, far as we can see it. Supposin' we believe the rest of the story.'

'About Ingels?' one of the others asked. 'Hell, Frank, that's too much to swallow!'

'Why is it? We know how close Ingels works

131

with Geis. And even if this Luke Barron is the
genuine article, the only thing we know about him
is that he's against Geis. Let's give him the benefit
of the doubt. If we do and if we're correct, him and
Randall's girl are in bad trouble. And Ingels has
our gold.'

'Suppose Barron was on his way out with the
gold for keeps and Geis found out about it,' another
suggested. 'He sent Ingels down to stop Barron and
save the ...'

'Wrong, you're dead wrong, Bert!' Summers cut
in. 'We tried to find Ingels before we left town. He
wasn't there. And he'd had plenty of time to show
up if he was goin' to. He wasn't at the hideout,
either. So what's your answer?'

Larsen put in, 'Looks like Tyler's story was
straight. If it was, we're wastin' time at this
palaverin'. We ought to be followin' out that sign.'

His words carried more weight than Summers',
for the argument had taken on the appearance of
Summers trying to convince his men against their
will. But as Larsen spoke, the last doubts of the
most sceptical were wiped out and all agreed to
head out on the sign.

They followed it up and out of Rattler and across
into the main canyon, where it struck north toward
town a quarter-mile and then climbed an obscure
trail to the rim. They rode the mesa past the town
and north beyond the line of the diggin's, losing the
sign completely as dusk began closing in on them.

When they halted and Bill Olds had made a wide cast across the nearby stretch of bare rock, he came back to tell them, 'We're licked. They didn't go on toward the hideout.' ... He nodded toward the west, and the horizon-reaching broken country off there. ... 'If they headed into that, we might as well give up. Nothin' to go on. Too much rock off there.'

'Then let's get back to town and see what we can pick up,' Summers suggested. 'Ingels won't dare be gone too long. We'll find him and put a couple men out to watch him. The same goes for Geis. We'll have to go about it careful, too. Nels, you and Bill and a few more heavy drinkers can hang out at the *Nugget* and go easy on the liquor. The rest of us'll loaf out along the street. How does it sound?'

'What about gettin' Randall in on this?' Olds asked. 'And Tyler. They could help.'

Summers nodded. 'We can pick 'em up on the way down.'

But George Randall's shack was empty and dark when they stopped there. It was decided finally not to wait for the prospector and the diggin's posse went on toward town, each man well posted on his particular chore for the next few hours.

Shortly after dark, Matt Geis heard a tapping on his office window, three quick knocks followed by two longer-spaced. He went to the window, opened it and saw Sam Ingels' face palely outlined against the darkened alley beyond.

'Everything go all right?' he queried, as the lawman passed two bulging heavy saddle-bags in to him.

Ingels nodded, the tight smile on his face giving Geis all the answer he needed.

'Better let yourself be seen on the street for an hour or two, Sam. Then get back here. Tell the boys to stay away until midnight.'

Ingels moved away in the darkness, Geis closed the window and knelt before the small safe in the back corner of the room, fiddling with the combination. He smiled broadly as he hefted the pouches, putting them into the safe. The safe locked again, he left the office and sauntered out through the crowded bar-room where the evening's business was at its heaviest.

Greeting acquaintances out there, he was affable, hearty. Against his habit, he accepted several invitations to drink. He spent an hour at the bar, until a warning signal in his mind told him he'd had enough whiskey for the moment. He went out the swing-doors onto the walk and stood leaning against the front wall of his saloon, eyeing the long line of people waiting at the water-valve, while a house-man served them and dropped his coins through the slitted top of the money-keg. Geis even smiled good-naturedly at the thought that his house-men must pocket some of that money. But tonight he didn't worry about it. Many nights it had taken two men to lift the solid weight of that money-filled keg and bring it in to be emptied before the early morning shift; what did he care about a few dollars lost when so much was rolling in?

He was feeling good tonight, the whiskey warming him and the knowledge of the young fortune in gold in his safe a reassuring thought. He'd be generous with his men, Ingels and his deputies, tonight. He wouldn't haggle over weighing out the gold. He'd even let Ingels take charge of that. A few ounces short of his half share of the yellow dust didn't matter.

Turning to re-enter the saloon, he happened to see Frank Summers standing at the edge of the walk, leaning against an awning-post. He pushed his way through the crowd to the claim-owner. He said, 'Come on in and have a drink with me, Frank.'

He caught Summers' quick look of belligerence and added: 'Hell, let's bury the hatchet, you and me! We're both in the same boat.'

Summers shook his head. 'No, we ain't, Geis. If I found myself in the boat with you, I'd jump overboard. And I can't swim.'

The saloon-owner's loose face took on an instant's cold anger, then broke into a smile. 'Suit yourself. Stage get through all right?'

'You ain't heard different, have you?'

Moving back to the *Nugget*'s doors, Geis spotted two more claim-owners loafing nearby. In a more sober mood, he wouldn't have noticed or thought anything peculiar in their being here; but now he happened to remember that one of the pair, Jeff Tolbert, wasn't a drinking man. Why, then, did Tolbert pick this crowded walk outside a saloon as a place to spend his time?

He thought about it on the way in and over another glass of rye at the bar. What he decided made him call one of the house-men across and tell him, 'Take a *pasear* around outside, Texas. See how many men from the diggin's you can spot, then get back here and tell me who they are and what they're doin'.'

Texas was gone ten minutes, so long that Geis's patience began to wear thin. He wasn't any longer in the mood for swapping talk with his customers, who seemed to pick this particular time to want to chin with him. When his house-man appeared, he nodded him back to the office and got his report in its privacy.

'Seven of 'em,' Texas told him and named five of Frank Summers' friends. 'Didn't know the others. There's at least four more milling around at the gamblin' layouts and the bar out there.' He jerked a thumb toward the door and the thin office partition through which came the din from the room beyond. 'Nothin' queer about that, is there?'

Geis frowned, a little worried but not showing

it. 'Get Ingels in here!' he told his man. 'Tell him to pick up as many of the boys as he can on his way. They're not to come in a bunch.'

EIGHTEEN

He had even a longer wait for his lawman to appear. When Ingels came in, he said, 'Looks like we've got trouble on our hands, Sam,' and was strangely irritated at the sheriff's obviously harried look.

At the bar out front, Bill Olds saw Bonanza's sheriff go into the rear office, followed several moments later by a pair of his deputies. On any other night, the appearance of these three wouldn't have aroused his curiosity. Now it did. He spent another ten minutes over a glass of beer and saw four more men unobtrusively enter Geis's office. Abruptly the two who had followed Ingels into the office came out and headed for the bar.

This pair, both wearing badges, held Olds' attention. When they came across to him and elbowed the bar to either side of him, he shot a quick glance toward the front poker layout, where Nels Larsen was looking in on the game. But Larsen wasn't looking his way and a slow feeling of foreboding settled through Olds.

He tossed a dollar onto the bar, told the apron, 'That's all for tonight, Ben.'

The apron pushed his change across the counter. As Olds reached out for it, the deputy on his left covered the money with his palm, drawling, 'Better stay and have another with us, Bill.'

The claim-owner gave the man a steady impassive look. 'I've had enough.'

'No, you ain't,' said the man on his right. 'You're buyin'. We're celebratin'.'

Olds' breath left his lungs in a long inaudible sigh. He could feel the perspiration standing out on his forehead. His palms were moist and there was a constriction in his throat as he forced a bleak smile. 'I'll have a beer, a short one.' He crossed his arms and leaned on the bar, feeling the prodding bulk of the .45 thrust through his belt under his coat. And now a slow anger was building up in him.

'Three whiskies, Ben,' the man with his hand on the money drawled. 'Olds is buyin'.' He pushed the claim-owner's change back across the bar.

The apron, uncorking a bottle of whiskey, looked down at the money and then at Olds. 'That ain't enough,' he said.

The deputy on his right looked at Olds. 'You heard what he said. He needs more money.'

The man's calm arrogance, his insolent smile,

suddenly brought Bill Olds' temper to the boiling point. He knew that these two were baiting him, looking for trouble. He knew, too, that he should be careful. He had one more visible danger signal as he glanced toward the back of the room, trying to spot another claim-owner who should be back there. Instead, he saw Matt Geis and Sam Ingels calmly regarding him from where they stood just outside the office door.

A quick panic took him. Yet he had the presence of mind to pretend to be reaching into his pocket as his right hand came down off the bar. Over his pocket, his hand hesitated an instant, then moved quickly, sweeping his coat aside and lifting toward the handle of his gun.

A man more practiced on the draw would have made good his chance. Olds didn't. The deputies to either side of him, reading his move an instant later, wheeled away, both reaching for their guns on the same instant. Olds' weapon was barely clear of his belt and he was turning to face the nearest man when a double concussion drove him hard against the bar.

One bullet took him in the side, another in the back. A hoarse scream welled up out of his throat, he clawed at the bar for support. Then, slowly, he folded to the floor. A last convulsion straightened him rigid as the customers to either side of the deputies crowded hurriedly out of the line of fire.

Across the room, Nels Larsen wheeled quickly

at the sound of the shots. He saw Bill Olds fall,
saw the smoking guns in the hands of the
deputies.

Without knowing how Olds had gotten into
trouble, knowing only that his friend lay there
dying, the Swede reached for the short-barrelled
.44 Smith and Wesson in his hip-pocket. No one
saw his move, for every eye in the room was
directed across there to the bar where Bill Olds
lay.

Larsen's gun settled into line with one deputy,
now stooping over Olds. He calmly squeezed the
trigger, saw his bullet knock the deputy off his
feet sideways, then brought the kicking weapon
into line with the second man. Close beside him,
one of the men at the poker layout fell backward
off his chair in a panic to get clear. Then Larsen
was firing again, coolly, his sights notched on the
second deputy's flat chest.

Pandemonium hit the *Nugget* at the instant of
the claim-owner's second shot. He had aimed
through a narrow aisle crowded on either flank
with the solid mass of the day's heaviest run of
customers. These now broke for the doors, wildly,
knocking each other down, trampling the unfor-
tunate bowled off their feet by those pressing from
behind. At the rear of the room, by the office door,
two shots beat the smoky air with a concussion
that made the lamps flicker. Larsen felt the
air-whip of a bullet hit his face and then he was

turning and running toward the nearest window, reaching for an over-turned chair and throwing it through the window ahead of him.

Back there was another shot and a lamp hanging from the ceiling shattered and went out. As Larsen stepped through the window, still another shot put out a second lamp. Outside, the old Swede ran down the narrow passageway toward the street. A staccato burst of uneven gun-fire rattled in the *Nugget*. The front window was smashed as Larsen came onto the walk and for a moment he was caught in the crowd wildly milling away from the saloon and out across the walk. The house-man who had been selling water had left his money-keg and was helplessly trying to push a way through to the doors.

Larsen spotted Frank Summers and Len Brown and Doc Savage crossing the street. They were running toward the opposite walk. He caught up with them as they made it and grabbed Summers by the arm, saying, 'Olds is dead. Couple of Ingels' men must've prodded him into goin' for his gun. I got the two that got him. Geis has half a dozen more men across there!'

They all looked across at the *Nugget* where the walk was now nearly clear. They were in time to see one of their men, Ned Wells, lunge out through the swing-doors and start across the walk. Suddenly a gun's flash lined out through the swinging doors and Wells missed his footing and fell face downward. He scrambled to his knees and was crawling to the walk's edge when that gun spoke again, its sharp explosion marking the instant the diggin's man went loosely onto his face again and lay still.

Frank Summers drew his gun and aimed at the doorway and emptied the weapon in a prolonged burst of sound. As he fired, the walk to either side of him and his companions emptied quickly into doorways and down the passageways between the buildings nearby. The last of his five bullets was ripping through the *Nugget*'s slatted door when a gun answered from the saloon's broken window. Summers took a staggering backward step as a bullet struck him in the right thigh. Then Doc Savage was reaching out, pulling him in toward the alleyway between two stores, saying sharply, 'Back, Frank!'

The four of them made the alleyway safely as other guns on the street took up the fight where Frank Summers had left it. The diggin's men had seen him and were grouping out front. Summers, clenching his leg, smiled grimly at the sound of those guns. The word must have travelled through the diggin's and he had more men than his original ten of this afternoon siding him now. These later recruits would have gone below, checked out their guns from the stand under the cottonwood and sneaked back into town, waiting for the trouble that was sure to break.

Summers turned to Larsen. 'Nels, hit the alleyways down from here and check on how many men we've got. I'll work up street. See if you can find Hardy and persuade him to open up the hardware-store. We need more guns and plenty of ...'

Savage said, 'You're going to stay here until we get this leg fixed, Frank.'

'Then you go, Len,' Summers said, speaking to the other man.

'How am I going to get Hardy to give us guns when there's a law against it?' Nels Larsen queried.

Frank Summers smiled thinly: 'We're the law here now. Tell Hardy that. Then get back and we'll fort up here in the pool-hall.'

NINETEEN

Coming into the head of the street, they could see the wink of the guns below coming from the *Nugget* and the windows of the stores opposite. The walks and even the street up here were crowded with watchers.

George Randall spotted a man he knew and called, 'What's up, John?'

'Shoot out. Bill Olds and Nels Larsen tackled a couple of Ingels' deputies. Bill cashed in, along with the deputies. Bunch o' your friends are swappin' lead with Geis and Ingels and their crowd now.' He waited until a sharp rattle of gunfire had died out. 'Looks like they was playin' for keeps!'

Luke said flatly, 'We'd better get down there.'

'Not you,' Randall told him. 'Remember, these so-called friends of mine are after your scalp. Wait here and I'll go down and see how things stand.'

'Me, too.' Ed Tyler swung from his saddle, following Randall's example. The two men handed their reins to Luke and Nancy and pushed out through the crowd.

'I hope he'll be careful,' Nan said and reined over closer to Luke. In the long interval that followed, he could tell from the expression on her face in the faint starlight that she was worried. He said, 'He'll be back.' But neither of them believed Randall would, for there had been something in the prospector's haste coming down the canyon, a look of unwary recklessness on his face even as he loaded a rifle before they left the shack, that told Luke that tonight represented the crisis of these long months of waiting for Nan's father. If Randall could join the fight down there, he wouldn't bother to come back and report.

Luke was impatient as he waited there, hearing the hushed and awed talk of the hundred or so spectators watching the fight nearby. At each renewed burst of the guns, at the high-pitched whine of the ricochetting bullets that droned up toward the rim, he sensed the danger represented by those men pitted against each other down the street. Men were being killed tonight, innocent men had already died. Somehow, the bunch from the diggin's that had set out on the trail of the stolen gold had found the right answer and come back to town tonight. But they'd been caught off guard and now, under the threat of those bullets from the *Nugget*, they were fighting against the heavy odds of Geis's trained gunmen. They did have a chance but it was a slim one.

Presently, it was obvious that the guns blazing out against the saloon were concentrated on the roof of a building directly opposite. Luke heard a man near him tell a neighbor, 'That's the stuff! They're usin' their heads, workin' from the roof of the pool-hall.'

In the statement, Luke found a voice for the sympathies of the crowd that obviously sided with the claim-owners but was wisely taking no part in their battle.

Barely a minute after the man had spoken, Luke felt Nan's hand take a grip on his arm. Then the girl was pointing down the street to something Luke had seen only a second ago.

'Fire!' someone shouted further along the street.

'Luke, they're caught!' Nan cried, and lifted her reins to push her pony on down the street. He reached out and stopped her.

In the windows of the buildings to either side of the one from which the claim-owners' guns were laying their bullets across at the *Nugget* glowed the tell-tale light of flames. The crowd saw it now and a hush settled along the street nearby. Suddenly a rifle far up toward the rim behind the street laid a sharply exploding fire down at the rear of the pool-hall where the claim-owners were holding out. Another joined it, then a third.

Someone on the walk across from Luke shouted, 'Geis has men up on the rim! The whole town'll burn!'

Luke said sharply, 'Wait here for me, Nan!' and stepped out of the saddle, dropping his reins and shouldering through the crowd toward the near walk. On the way there, he spoke to men he passed, 'Come along with me. You, too! Hurry! Get the big fellow across there!'

On the walk across from the *Nugget* and a hundred yards short of the saloon, he told nearly twenty men who had gathered around him: 'Get buckets, all you can find! Put some men on the roofs above and below those fired buildings and run your bucket-line down from the ditch. You'll have to work fast if you're going to keep this thing from spreading!'

'How the hell will Summers and his crowd get out?' one man asked him.

'They'll get out!' he told them. 'Get a move on!'

His way of speaking carried a force they could believe in. As they scattered on the run, calling back to the crowd for volunteers to form a bucket-line down from the ditch that ran along the east wall above the street, Luke turned and went along toward the burning buildings. At each step he could feel a jarring pain in his shoulder.

Smoke was billowing out onto the street in a thick cloud. A moment ago he'd had an idea that meant the end of waiting. As he hurried his stride, he palmed the .45 from the holster at his thigh.

Suddenly, out of the fog of smoke fifty yards ahead staggered a man at a run. He had taken three steps into the clear, beyond the screening smoke, when the guns across at the *Nugget* opened up on him. Luke saw the bullets hit, saw the man's body jerk even as he fell. He rolled to the edge of the walk and lay there, head and shoulders on the planking, boots in a puddle of muddy water at the gutter. He was dead before his body stopped its roll.

Luke halted abruptly, wheeling into a store doorway. In that still figure on the walk he saw the blasting of his one hope to reach the pool-hall and help George Randall and Ed Tyler and the claim-owners. The thought he'd had a moment ago was to take his chances on being hidden by the smoke. Now he saw that a light breeze blowing up-canyon was thinning the veil of smoke enough for the *Nugget* men to spot any man moving close to the pool-hall along the walks.

The rifles from the rim behind the street cut loose in a sharp racketing fire. Grimly, Luke realized that the claim-owners were trapped. Their guns didn't count now. All Geis had to do was keep the pool-hall covered from the front and back until the fire drove the claim-owners into the open. Then Randall and his friends would have a choice. They could either throw down their guns and come out with hands up or make a running fight of it, a fight that couldn't but end in one way. There were too many guns against them to make this one way doubtful.

As though to prove Luke's thought, he heard Matt Geis's booming voice call across from the *Nugget*: 'Toss your guns onto the street and come out reachin', you pack o' sand-grubbers!'

And, answering the taunting order, came George Randall's cry, 'Like hell we will!' followed by a furious blast that raked the front of the saloon.

'Go on! Waste your lead, Randall!' Geis called back. 'When you've had enough, sing out!'

The only answer the saloon-owner received this time was from the guns. Their blasting chatter marked the ending of Luke's hope.

Across there, backed by his guns, was a man into whose merciless grip this boom-town would fall before the night was out. Matt Geis, the man who had bought the law, whose deputies were the only men allowed to carry guns within the town limits, would tomorrow make his own terms for bringing peace to Bonanza. What law there was would be his law from now on.

Luke's glance went up to the far rim, where, barely visible in the light of the burning buildings below, stood Matt Geis's huge water-tank. It was a squatting bulk held upright by sturdy timbered legs, a dark shadow hanging over the town at the head of the narrow gully down which its pipe-line ran to the rear of the *Nugget*.

Suddenly, flattened in the protection of the doorway, Luke had a thought that made him

150

wheel quickly out onto the walk and turn back up-street at a run. A lone bullet challenged his going, knocking a splinter from a plank a foot behind one boot. He ignored it, glancing down the passageways between the stores to see the bucket-line being formed on the wall-slope beyond the back alley. He came to the fringes of the crowd and left the walk, moving across the street to where he saw Nan's slender shape over the others.

He swung up onto his pony, wheeled the animal around, calling to her, 'Come along.' They left the end of the street at a run, Luke swinging sharply left toward the west wall of the canyon. As he rode, he was untying the rope from his saddle-horn, calling to the girl, 'Can you get me to the top of the rim?'

She swung sharply away from him, up the steep loose talus-slope. He followed, admiration filling him at the blind faith of this girl, whose father was trapped between two burning buildings down the street, yet who didn't hesitate an instant now. Another woman would have wanted to know what he was doing. But Nan only pushed on, punishing her pony to keep him on his feet up across the loose rock and then threading her way between the huge slabs of rock that lay below the rim.

TWENTY

They climbed eternally, or so it seemed to Luke, turning back away from town then swinging sharply on a line parallel with the street. But they were gaining on those fifty feet that separated them from the rim. Once Nan's horse slipped and went to his knees. She had him on his feet again before Luke could pull alongside to help.

They made the rim with their ponies badly blown. But Luke didn't stop, taking the lead now and striking down toward the towering shadow of Matt Geis's water-tank and its neighboring windmill.

He drew rein close in to one of the four two-foot-thick timber supports, flicking his rope to widen the noose. He turned to face the girl and saw that she was untying the rope from her saddle.

'Think it'll work?' he asked and had his answer in a nod of her head. She had been quick to see what he intended doing.

He spent precious moments scooping the drifted sand from the base of the nearest support with his hands. Finally he had cleared the concrete base on which the butt end of the log rested. At that moment he saw for the first time a complication in the two long bolted rods that ran crosswise between the timbers, holding them together at a slight outward angle. The rods were of half-inch iron, capped with washers and a bolt.

She saw him kneeling there, looking at the bolt that held the big timber rigid, locked to the obliquely opposite support. 'Could you shoot it off?' she asked. He gave her a grateful look, drew his gun and carefully sent two bullets crashing against the bolt. The second bullet broke the bolt-end. The rod, its end released, sang with the slacked tension and pulled clear of the hole and fell to the ground.

He tied the end of the two ropes around the butt end of the support. He handed Nan the end of one, stepped into the saddle and wound the end of the other around the horn.

He said, 'When this thing cuts loose, make tracks away from here,' and she nodded, following his example and easing her pony into the pull gently, to avoid weakening the rope.

In those brief moments in which his pony strained against the dead weight of the rope, Luke glanced across at Nan and then down the line of the deep gully and at the street far below. The

Nugget's rear wall made a grey splash in the shadows down there. Beyond, the street was filled with a drifting cloud of smoke, the pool-hall barely in sight through it. But the two burning buildings flanking it made bright scars of light. He could see the men at the ends of the bucket-lines frantically emptying buckets of water across the neighboring roofs. And as he watched he saw a sudden burst of flame come alive on the pool-hall roof. There wasn't much time left.

Suddenly, his pony took a long uncertain forward step. There was a creaking and a groaning of timbers behind. His glance swept around to the tank's huge bulk, towering high overhead. Then, with an explosion like the thunder of artillery, the butt end of the huge log support left its concrete base and shot outward.

'Run!' he shouted, but already Nan's spurs had gouged her pony's flanks, lifting him to a reaching lope.

They stopped and turned their ponies a hundred feet out from the tank in time to see it topple slowly inward toward the nearby rim. Its wooden seams parted, the iron rods snapped apart, and five thousand gallons of water burst outward and hit the rim with an earth-jarring drive. The water geysered upward in a tall plume, then plummeted downward and out of sight.

Fascinated, they rode to the rim and looked downward. A raging foaming wall of water was sweeping down the steep gully toward the back of the *Nugget*, carrying boulders and uprooted cedars before it. It swept onward majestically, slowly but relentlessly with a roar that drowned out the sound of the guns and seemed to shake the rimrock.

As the last of that rush of water drained off the rim, Luke said quickly, 'Get down there and wait, Nan.' Then he was prodding his pony's flanks, sending the animal down over the rim's edge and into the bottom of the downward-sloping gully. The horse, panicked, slid and ran down the gully with a swiftness that overtook the last trickle of rushing water.

Luke saw that solid wall of water foam up out of the gully's end, smash apart a lean-to and then hit the back wall of the saloon. The thin frame wall stood up under the drive of the water for a split-second only, then tore inward to let the tons of water through. Luke heard a man scream out over the thunder of the avalanche. Then he was crossing the back alley with his pony at a run, aiming for the twenty-foot hole torn in the *Nugget*'s wall.

He went through it with his .45 aiming a chattering blast at the huge opening in the front wall where the water had swept away half the saloon's face. A man up there was struggling knee-deep in water, holding to the torn end of a two-by-four wall support. One of Luke's bullets broke his hold and he was swept out of sight in the rush of water onto the street. Off to Luke's left, a gun lanced a crimson stab of flame that brought his pony down. As he vaulted from the saddle, he targeted that flame-stab and thumbed a single shot. He heard a choked cry of pain, then the thud of a body as he side-stepped toward one darkened wall, shucking fresh loads from his belt.

Directly across the room toward the bar, he heard an object fall to the floor. Then a boot scraped across there. He picked out the outline of the huge bar-mirror on the opposite wall as guns set up an uneven chant of explosions out on the street. In the mirror he could see the reflected face of the pool-hall through the torn out front of the saloon. Men were pouring out the pool-hall door across the street, running along the opposite walk. He recognized George Randall among them, and saw Randall stop and take aim with a six-gun and fire down along the clean-swept street.

Then, before those reflected images, moved a bigger and a closer figure. Luke instantly recognized Matt Geis's massive frame. The *Nugget* owner was standing across there by his overturned bar, in front of the mirror.

Luke laid his sights on Geis's wide chest, then lowered his gun. This was cold-blooded murder, even if the man he was killing deserved no chance. He stood there, trying to think of a way of taking Geis alive, when all at once he saw the saloon-owner's arm lift a gun into line with him.

In a split-second, he realized that he was out-lined by the light of the burning buildings reflected through a side window at his back. He lunged as Geis's gun exploded at him. Then, arcing up his own weapon, he thumbed the .45 empty. As the repeated pound of the weapon travelled along his arm, he was only vaguely aware of the answering shots, of a burning pain along one thigh, of a tug at his shirt.

All he knew was that Geis, outlined before the mirror, was staggering back under a solid blow each time his gun exploded. Five times he dis-tinctly saw the impact of his bullets as they slammed into the big man. Five times he expected Geis to go down off his feet and five times Geis remained standing after that jerk of his huge frame.

The hammer of Luke's .45 clicked on an empty shell. All at once a lantern's flickering light moved into the torn-out front wall of the saloon. At the corner of his vision, Luke sensed the presence of men up there, many men. But he was watching Geis as the lantern-light fell full on him.

Matt Geis stood there staring across at Luke, eyes wider than Luke had ever seen them. The saloon-owner's white-shirted chest was torn by holes that could have been covered by the spread of a man's hand; it was stained darkly with crimson. Beyond lay the overturned bar and at his feet was a

157

litter of broken bottles and glasses.

Suddenly Geis made a last effort to raise the gun hanging in his hand at his side. He had lifted it halfway into line when he tottered sideways, slowly, reminding Luke of the ponderous fall of the water-tank on the rim a few moments ago. He fell stiffly, face downward into a mass of broken glass.

Someone behind Luke said, 'Goddlemighty! It's Barron!'

He turned slowly to face the men at the front as George Randall and Ed Tyler pushed into the littered opening in the front wall.

Ed wheeled to face the men up there, a gun in his hand. 'Back, damn it! Back before I let this thing off!'

A man Luke had never seen before, Frank Summers, told Ed, 'No one wants Barron, Tyler. Hell, didn't he just save our necks? Hasn't he got a pardon waitin' him in Texas?'

Hours afterward, when they all gathered on the walk before the *Nugget* after battling the fires across the street with buckets and axes and dynamite, George Randall said wearily, 'Our gold ought to be in Geis's safe, according to Luke. See if you can find it in that mess inside.'

Frank Summers and Nels Larsen went in through the torn out front of the saloon, picking their way through the litter of broken tables and chairs and jagged-end boards lying strewn across

158

the floor. The *Nugget* had been completely gutted by the flood of water that had poured through it and gone rushing off down the canyon.

Ed Tyler, coming across after helping the crew over there water the last smouldering embers of the two burned buildings, asked Randall, dismally, 'Where's Luke?' He was looking at the blanket-draped shapes nearby on the walk, the bodies of four dead claim-owners.

'Saw him across here with Nan a minute ago,' Randall said. He saw that Ed, like himself and all these others who had battled the flames, was worn out and dead for sleep. But even though he was dog-tired, Randall could smile as he said, 'Wonder what chances we have of gettin' Luke to stay on as sheriff?'

Ed looked surprised. 'Reckon you ought to give Nan the job of askin' him, George.'

In the shadow of the awning twenty feet down the walk, Nan looked up into Luke's face and her hand tightened the hold of his arm about her waist. They hadn't spoken for long minutes, too sobered by the destruction around them to break the silence.

'What chances are there, Luke?' Nan whispered suddenly. 'Will you stay?'

'Would you like bein' a sheriff's wife?'

'If you're the sheriff.'

An interruption came then as Frank Summers led his men out onto the walk, holding a paper out to Randall. 'Here's something you lost a while back, George,' the claim-owner drawled.

'What is it?'

'The deed for those claims of yours. I think if you paid a lawyer about a dollar, we could make the transfer legal in your name. We'll throw in Geis's well, too, and you can give it to the town and help Savage clean out this typhoid.'

Ed Tyler saw Nels Larsen come out of the saloon behind Summers. Larsen was carrying the saddle-bags that held the gold.

'That about clears everything up, don't it? Wonder where that side-kick of mine is?' He called loudly, 'Hey, Luke!'

'Let him howl,' Luke said low-voiced to Nan.

'Yes,' she whispered, and tilted her face up to his kiss.